The Skating Pond

The Skating Pond

Deborah Joy Corey

Thorndike Press • Chivers Press
Waterville, Maine USA   Bath, England

This Large Print edition is published by Thorndike Press®, USA and by Chivers Press, England.

Published in 2003 in the U.S. by arrangement with The Berkley Publishing Group, a member of Penguin Group (USA) Inc.

Published in 2003 in the U.K. by arrangement with the author.

U.S. Hardcover 0-7862-5452-1 (Core Series)
U.K. Hardcover 0-7540-7236-3 (Chivers Large Print)
U.K. Softcover 0-7540-7237-1 (Camden Large Print)

The first chapter of *The Skating Pond* appeared in a slightly different form as "The Skating Pond" in the *Carolina Quarterly*.

The text of this Large Print edition is unabridged.
Other aspects of the book may vary from the original edition.

Set in 16 pt. Plantin by Minnie B. Raven.

Printed in the United States on permanent paper.

British Library Cataloguing-in-Publication Data available

Library of Congress Cataloging-in-Publication Data

Corey, Deborah Joy, 1958–
    The skating pond / Deborah Joy Corey.
        p. cm.
    ISBN 0-7862-5452-1 (lg. print : hc : alk. paper)
    1. Women — Maine — Fiction.   2. Fishing villages — Fiction.   3. Loss (Psychology) — Fiction.   4. Maine — Fiction.   5. Large type books.   I. Title.
    PR9199.3.C6525S58 2003b
    813′.54—dc21   2003045883

WILDERMUTH

For my mother

Your brain in love remains a sacred, suffo-
cating swamp . . .

— Natalie Angier

Part One

1

Sometimes I see my mother skating across the pond with her arms like outstretched wings. Her long hair that never separated sways in the air with the glow of coal and moonlight and she is always smiling, her white teeth hiding her lower lip.

I was fourteen when we stopped going to the pond and the memories are no longer clear to me, but come back slowly in dots and gentle colors as if I am watching Seurat paint. This happens when I am alone, sitting at my kitchen table and looking out over the marsh where cranes swoop and disappear in the long heady grass. The trees are bare black around the circle of the marsh, and in bright sunlight everything has its own course of movement. The marsh grass moves with the most grace — sometimes sullen like a stream as if the day is sultry and then without warning, waving at me, skittishly and with great humor. January is when I think of her most, when the weather has stolen all there is to steal and the earth looks barren under cold blue skies, as if waiting.

The year was 1968 and home was an old two-storey house perched on a jagged hill of granite overlooking Stonington Harbor in Maine. The harbor was filled with lobster boats and islands that were covered in undulating hills of pine and spruce and fir trees. Across the way sat Crotch Island where they quarried a sandy-rose granite called "Sherwood Pink." Jacqueline Kennedy had chosen it for her husband's memorial stone, compelling Mother to say that all things beautiful had to leave this place. I wondered then if *this place* was Stonington or the very earth we all inhabited. Mother was from eastern Canada and her dislike for Stonington was drawn as firmly as the border between the two countries. To her, it was a place of old ways and unwritten rules, a place with no interest in anything new or exotic. Whenever she said this, I thought of the town cemetery on the rocky hill with tombstones in memory of seafaring men who died on the coast of Africa or lost their lives at sea in China and East India. Perhaps those men had felt the same way Mother did. Perhaps staring at the sea made people restless. Often, I felt threatened that Mother would someday leave Stonington to search for something more, just as those men had. I pictured her beauty embodied in a figurehead at the front of a great ship, flying fearlessly above treacherous waters.

After school, Mother stood at the door with a piece of cheddar cheese for me. "Eat it quickly while you put your ski pants on."

She walked impatiently from the square maple table that sat in the middle of our kitchen to the sink and then to the window with her skates hanging over her shoulder, one at her chest and the other one resting on her back like a broken wing. She was dressed in black ski pants and a black jacket. A pink wool hat circled her face and brought out the blush of her skin.

Father was in his room off the kitchen that faced south, painting. It was once the bedroom of my dead grandfather, but had long been transformed. Or maybe it would be better to say the very memory of my grandfather was painted over a thousand times. The oily smell of turpentine and cigarettes rode in waves through the house and the slapping of Father's brushes sounded like small feet rushing over wet rocks. "Doreen," he said, "maybe Elizabeth doesn't want to go skating every day after school."

His voice came from all directions, first deep and then hanging in the air like something that had sprung from the bottom of the sea. I pictured Father squinting at the painting on his easel, his smooth red scalp shining through his dark brush cut, his thick neck muscles tight and tense-looking. He was doing an oil painting of a boy searching a rocky shore and for a moment, while I chewed my cheese, I thought how nice it

11

would be if he painted me instead of the boy. "Elizabeth can stay with you if she wants to," Mother said.

The winter sunlight was orange on the walls. Outside, bare tree branches blew, making a shadow of swords on the floor. Father's voice turned low and steady. "I'm working."

Mother looked off toward his room tapping her long fingers on her ski pants. "Hurry, Elizabeth," she said. "It will be dark before we get there."

I stepped behind the wood stove where the skates hung on hooks like sails set to dry. My older sister Gwen's skates lay beneath mine. It was all I could do to keep from grabbing them and holding them up like a bird shot from the sky. Wasted. Father had sent Gwen away two years earlier for what he called inappropriate behavior with an Italian quarryman. Now, she lived three hours south in Belfast with Father's sister, Marie. Mother often drove down for the day, but Father never allowed me to go, contending that Gwen was a bad example and heading for a life of trouble.

"She's my sister," I always said, but those words were as weightless as the foamy white bubbles that sometimes gathered in the harbor and disappeared.

Father came and stood in his doorway. He

was thick with an abundant face that reddened when he painted. Around him were always shadows as if he'd deliberately painted them to keep us from ever seeing him clearly. He squinted one eye while the smoke rose from the cigarette at the corner of his straight mouth. He wiped his hands with a white rag, then inhaled hard and plucked the cigarette from his closed lips. "I'm sorry, Elizabeth."

Sorry? How are you sorry? It appeared that *sorry* was a word that allowed people to misbehave, a safety net much like the act of confession. My ski pants hissed as I moved toward the door. "I want to go anyway," I said, stepping outside.

"Perfect day for the pond." Mother breathed. Her emerald eyes were searching the suddenly sunless sky.

"What are you looking for?" I asked.

"Seagulls," she said.

Sometimes if it was going to storm, the white birds came inland and swooped about the houses and yards. They were partial to our area because several fields behind the village, near the cemetery, was a public dump. "Father says they're scavengers," I said, "and that I shouldn't go near them."

Mother stopped and looked at me. "That is so silly."

"But they eat garbage, Mother."

"Of course they do. It's their purpose.

They keep the harbor clean."

She walked quickly down our short road and up Route 15, turning at the Square Deal Garage and along Indian Point Road. Two men working in the yard at the Lobster Co-Op waved, but Mother didn't wave back. She was moving toward the frozen lily pond as if it were calling her. So smoothly, as if she were already wearing her skates.

In the summer, tourists came to the pond early in the morning to see the lilies before they closed for the day, but the pond belonged to the locals in the winter, especially to Mother and to the fishermen's sons who had a hockey team called Seamen Steamers. Years later, while reminiscing, Gwen would laugh, *Semen Steamers, you can say that again.* The memory of her remark ignited a warm and youthful picture, the shimmering peachy hair on her tanned arms and her broad flat feet with pubescent toenails painted Coral Kiss, not in the knowing way of a seductress, but in the curious and adventurous way of a woman-child. Now I picture girls at that age as being blindfolded, stumbling into womanhood. So much depends on their leader.

Mother and I put our skates on in the warming shed. Before going out to the ice, I stood in front of the potbelly stove and warmed myself. The shed was always hot and smelled of dry burning wood and dirt. The

14

dirt smell surprised me because the little oblong-shaped building always seemed to be swept clean. A half dozen small square windows faced the pond and were covered with chicken wire. I often watched Mother from those windows and felt imprisoned, not by the wire, but by her smooth beauty and fearlessness. Watching her, I wished to skate as strongly, wished to be as brave.

There were a lot of mothers at the pond with their children, but most of them didn't skate. They talked inside the shed or stood at the edge of the pond where the ice was opaque and broken. My mother skated in a fury, frontward and backward, chopping up the ice with spins and stretching herself in midair splits. She had taught herself to do all of this. Her skates were solid custom boots she'd had made by a man in Montreal when she was eighteen. There was no doubting her dream when you watched her. The boys who played hockey at one end of the pond often stopped to watch, leaning their chins on top of their sticks, their bright woolen scarves blowing in the wind. Skating was my mother's point of genius. She could watch a spin being done on television and do it herself the following day at the pond. Once, a man who was visiting Stonington watched Mother skating and told her she should join the Ice Capades. He said he even knew someone if she would consider it, but Father

15

said no. I believe he said, "Aren't we enough for you?"

Stepping on the pond, I noticed a red mitten frozen under the ice. It lay flat and I almost expected to see a small hand come up from the black abyss and place itself in the mitten. There was a whole other world at the pond. Fall leaves trapped as if in glass, white puffy blotches that were sealed, but had a sort of still movement like cumulus clouds that had fallen from the sky.

I was a toe picker and as I picked off toward my mother, she said loudly, "Make T's, Elizabeth. Don't use those picks. Use the edge of your blades." All the clattering of hockey sticks, the swishing of skates and the blend of ice-bound voices disappeared and I was at once lost with the missing sounds, making my way to my mother, her back arched and her mouth open in expectation.

"Watch me," she said, grabbing my arm and bringing me to a complete stop before I slid into her. I stood, my legs bent, my arms hanging down toward the ice, long and stiff like a monkey's.

Mother made perfect T's across the pond, sliding one blade out to the side and bringing the other foot in to make the T again, a slow bounce in her body as if she were hurrying to escape. When she was bored of T's, she gained speed and near the edge of the pond where old hay sprang from

16

the snow, she jumped and split in the air, touching the toe of each skate with her fingers. I looked down at the ice and it was sheer black except for a small broken twig and the T prints my mother's skates had made.

"Can you do that?" Julie Ann Sparrow asked. She was standing right beside me when I looked up. "Can you do a jump like your mother?" Her cheeks were red and dry from the wind.

"It's called a *sow-cow*," I said. "And you know I can't."

We both watched as Mother skated toward us, her body growing tall and straighter with closeness. She circled us fast in the finest display of crossovers I had ever seen. When Mother skated, she looked like something from a fairy tale, a gazelle, thin-necked and elegant. "Gee," Julie Ann breathed, "she sure is good."

"She's had a lot of practice," I said.

Julie Ann rubbed her runny nose with her mitten and nodded her head. "Yep, my mother says she's always here doing her circles."

I pictured Julie Ann's mother, a heavy woman who packed sardines at The Lubec Canning Company. Often, she still wore the mandatory black hair net while she shopped at Bartlett's market after her shift. Her face was both bloated and fleshy, but her gray eyes were as warm as polished stones. Her words were warm and worn, too, but somehow cunning like the very clichés and scoldings that eventually made Julie Ann somewhat suspicious of everyone. Later in life, Julie Ann would be wilder than any girl I knew. Who could blame her? All those sayings tick, tick, ticking in her head: *We reap what we sow. You make your bed, you sleep in it. Every man gets married with his zipper down.* . . . In time, I guess the ticking subsided, but a time of wildness seemed necessary to hush the steady beating in Julie Ann's head, ordaining her as the easy girl, the one capable of fulfilling any boy's fantasy.

A number of times Julie Ann invited me to her house, but Father never allowed me to go, because Mr. Sparrow raised Eskimo dogs. Father said they were notorious for biting children's faces, but maybe he hated the dogs because they originated in Canada, the land that according to my mother was the land of freedom, or perhaps it was that the dogs were originally bred with wolves, or maybe it was that we once had a dog named Sadie, whose life had ended tragically. Once, when a particularly large litter was born, I begged Father to let me have one. He said, "Elizabeth, they are pack dogs by nature and they will always squabble for seniority."

"But I only want one dog," I said. "Who will it squabble with here?" He threw his arms up and walked away, shaking his head. *Why didn't I understand they couldn't be trusted?*

Julie Ann and I met at Austin's Dock or in front of Sparky's canteen and wandered about town. Sometimes while wandering, I pictured myself being attacked by one of her dogs, pictured it devouring my face. I was at that age where horrid fantasies of destruction counteract the reality of parental control. Yes, a girl without a face. That would get some sympathy from my parents. Nothing where the eyes and nose and mouth should be. Just a mangled face. Later, when my face was much older, I found a faceless Amish doll in a shop. While touching it, I wept with the sounds of a young girl, running from the shop girl's questioning eyes. I am still haunted by that doll's blank face, its history so well defined by what is missing.

At home, Father had started supper, but Mother only wanted cinnamon toast and a glass of milk. Father said something about Canadians and their toast, but before it could turn into an argument, I said, "I'll eat macaroni and tomatoes."

Father was at the window by the sink where his paint brushes were lined in jars of milky turpentine. Those were the brushes he used to paint the fishing boats. He said boats were not what he really wanted to paint, but fishermen constantly banged on our door asking Father to do them the favor. That winter he had already painted a *Margaret Jean* and *Lillian Mary*, the *Margaret Jean* having been banged to bits and pieces on the rocky banks of the shore when it broke loose in a storm. Father always painted the fishing boats in dangerous waters. No wonder fishermen wanted his paintings. Who doesn't love a story of danger, particularly if it is your own and you have survived.

My grandfather died at sea while he and Father were lobstering. It was 1954, the year I was born, and Hurricane Edna was beginning to whip up the seas. A white wave took Grandfather from the stern of the boat. After that, Father hated the sea. He said it was an unpredictable force with the personality of a shark, swallowing whatever was in front of it whether it was hungry or not. Apparently, Grandfather had been swept away in a matter of seconds. Father never spoke of him again. He made Grandfather's bedroom into his painting room, then painted a multitude of empty and abandoned fishing boats. When I was five, I suggested he try painting something different and his mood turned dark. Years later I would see a painting by the Maine painter John Marin, in which the sun was black on white canvas, its contrast so intense with the white that it gave the effect of burning through the paper. My father's darkness could burn through me, too, making me as insignificant as a pile of ashes.

If skating was my mother's toehold on youth, then painting was Father's toehold on death. I believe he was trying to resurrect his father by painting those fishing boats. Sometimes, if he finished a particularly tattered boat, one that looked as if it had gone to the bottom of the sea and back, he became almost giddy. He idealized his world on the flat plane of a canvas, and for a time that seemed to give him the control he so desired.

Beside my plate at the supper table was a pencil sketch. It was on a three-by-five piece of white paper and in the picture I was glancing downward with my thin lips in a satisfied curve. Father must have made some mistake, for the portrait was neither me nor not me. It was somewhere in between, like the photograph of a baby in a womb, bland but somehow individual. "What about the boy on the rocky shore?" I asked.

"He's finished," Father said, sitting down at his place. Mother was sprinkling her toast with cinnamon and sugar and the kitchen smelled of Christmas. She licked the corners of her mouth, savoring the sweet specks. "Peter," she said, "when are you going to do me skating?"

Father's face lost its expression. He was not partial to Mother's skating. Once, while they argued about her preoccupation with the pond, he said, "People see it as decadence, Doreen. You have a home and a family. You should be here." He was lying on the kitchen couch and dust particles were rolling in the white rays of sunlight near his wool socks. He was reading a tattered book.

Mother was sitting at the table looking at pictures of Peggy Fleming, who had just won a gold medal at the Olympics. "What?" she said.

Father repeated himself and Mother slapped her magazine shut, staring at him. Father looked at her for a moment, then threw his book, which only grazed her and landed beside my feet, where I stood looking over her shoulder. Mother got up and marched off while I picked the book up and looked inside. The corner was turned down on a center page and I read, "And had you watched Ahab's face that night, you would have thought that in him also two different things were warring."

After supper, I ripped the sketch of myself in two and placed it between the pages of my prayer book. It was windy and the windows rattled. Frost had made shapes like faces on the pane. I put my fingers on the smallest face to melt eyes, then pulled them back, wet and cold. I imagined the distant breakers where salty seawater rose and turned white and waves twisted and crashed and rolled against the islands. Sometimes when we watched the wild sea, Father said she was having a temper tantrum and all anyone could do was wait until it was over. With these words he sounded helpless, as helpless as a man watching a loved one being swallowed by a wave.

The face that Father sketched was of an older me. Of all his qualities, intuition was the strongest. He could look at something and know what time was capable of doing to it. When he painted any person, you could see how well he understood their essential framework, and on their skeleton he hung their future: saggy expressions, slouching shoulders, and protruding bellies. Perhaps that is why people asked for paintings of boats instead of portraits of themselves.

On Saturday night of that week, we all went to the pond. Father took his sketch pad and Mother and I took our skates. There was a line of lightbulbs on wire strung across the pond and the lights were lit and swaying. The night was deep navy blue everywhere except for the rink where the lights and wind made a yellow moving glow over the ice. A large speaker on top of the skating shed played Patsy Cline's "Crazy."

Mother was wearing white tights and a white skating skirt. She had sewn silver sequins to the hem and it sparkled when she moved. The shed was full of people, and all types and sizes of boots were piled and spilling from under the benches. Father helped me tighten my skates while Mother raced to get outside. "Does she ever wait for you?" he said in an accusing way. I shrugged, chewing the end of my mitten. Father's black whiskers poked from his face. He asked again, but I said nothing.

When we stepped outside, Mother was up near the boys playing hockey. She was doing backward crossovers in a huge private circle. Julie Ann was there and so I skated off with her, picks first, while Father sat on the new snow at the edge of the pond and began to sketch. Occasionally, he looked up to find Mother or me, but mostly he just made little thrusting movements with his pencil and greeted familiar faces as they skated by. Once, when Julie Ann and I were going by, she yelled, "What are you drawing, Mr. Johnson?"

He looked up and smiled. "A boat."

I was taken aback because I pictured a skating scene with recognizable figures. "Elizabeth," he called out, "don't go near the edges of the pond. It may not be frozen."

Julie Ann looked at me and lifted one eyebrow. A cold snap had left the temperature below freezing for days. I ignored her expression and skated off toward Mother. Julie Ann followed and there seemed to a be a small apology in her enthusiasm to keep up.

I didn't want to get too close to Mother fearing that she'd correct me on my T pushoffs. Julie Ann and I made a spot for ourselves in the center of the pond where the ice was white and it was hard to believe that somewhere under us water flowed and lilies waited to bloom again. There were a lot of girls with their boyfriends. They skated around the edge hand in hand. "Do you think they kiss?" Julie Ann said pointing to a couple with matching cableknit sweaters.

"I don't know," I said, and Julie Ann slipped her mitten in mine as if somewhere in the quietest parts of ourselves, we were making a similar silent wish.

I don't think Father was looking when Mother got hit with the puck, but I heard something. I believe it was the cracking of her forehead. They said she was spinning so fast that the sequins on her skirt looked like neon and that when the puck struck her, all her bones seemed to dissolve and she fell like cloth to the ice. The first thing I saw was Father running across the pond and the skaters moving with him like lemmings racing for the sea. Someone scratched the needle across the record and the speaker blared out a ripping sound. The night was just cold weather touching us with the sound of lightbulbs swinging in the wind and the scraping of blades on the ice. Julie Ann and I were still holding hands and she began to pull me toward Mother. Instantly, my legs and arms swelled with weight and something that weighed like a heavy black stone grew in my chest.

The puck had hit Mother between her eyes. One side of her face was pressed hard against the ice. A slender white bone jutted out between her eyebrows and dark blood gushed from the split it made. Father lifted Mother up. The violet-colored blood poured from the cut and her nose in a steady stream to the ice. I stood in the circle of skaters away from them. There was a lot of staring and whispering. The lights made swinging shadows across Mother's face and there was so much blood that I thought it must be seeping up from the pond. The sequins lay like a silver snake on her legs and one of her thigh muscles was pulsating. A young boy with a navy face mask began to cry. Julie Ann looked at me and I smiled, my body somehow separate from my feelings.

When the sled arrived, Father put his hand out and held everyone at bay. "Doreen," he said, "can you hear me?"

Mother's eyes stayed closed but her mouth fell open in an O, the slack-jaw hollow O of opaque. Father wiped the blood away from her lips and underneath they were the softest color of pink, like the tongue of an infant. A breath of white escaped her and rose up to Father. For a moment, he closed his eyes and it looked as if they were both sleeping. When he opened them, the creases in his face had grown deeper like ruts in a heavily traveled road. He touched the swelling over her eyes, which made her forehead sway like water. "I'll put her on," he said.

We all watched, waiting for some sign of life to come from Mother and when she revealed nothing, we became a parade following the sled across the ice.

Back in the shed, everyone gathered to wait for the ambulance to come from Blue Hill. Father never took his eyes off Mother. He held his brown woolen glove to her nose and head to stop the bleeding and it was wet and dripping like a sponge. Blades banged gently on the wooden floor making a dull sound that beat at the black stone inside of me. Everyone was huddled around the sled that held Mother and once in a while someone would touch me on the back to comfort me. At the time, Mother didn't look enough like herself for me to cry, but I did wish hard for Father to kiss her.

"Could you clear the shed?" Father said. Mother had not moved and the curtness in his voice probably came from the worry that she might not. He wrapped his hand around her baby finger that stood in the air and squeezed it. Whispers carried the skaters in a slow exit and I was moved with them back out to the pond.

Mother was in Blue Hill Hospital for one night, then transferred to St. Joseph's Hospital in Bangor, where she stayed for three and a half weeks. When we brought her home, her nose was flat and her once almond-shaped eyes seemed to have been traded in for wider ones. Her forehead was sunken like the dip over a grave and her face was still swollen and blue. Much later in life, I would see pictures of children who suffered from fetal alcohol syndrome and be reminded of Mother. When Mother wandered about the house, I stood out of her way as if she were a stranger.

"Elizabeth," she said. "Are you afraid of me now?" She was unscrewing the mirror from her dresser and I was sitting on the bed, watching my reflection. "No," I said, not really sure if I was or not. My long and wild hair blazed black in the sunlight, but my lips looked wispy and pale like the cirrus clouds that come before a warm front.

"Don't be afraid," she said. "Nothing has changed."

I wanted to cry, but instead I turned to the window. It was a calm cold day and a row of icicles hung there. They were lavender in the bright light, the very lavender of summer lupines and there were a thousand tiny bubbles trapped in their frozen surface. I looked back. "Is your face going to get better?"

Mother rested the round mirror up against her thighs and it made a circle of dust on her jeans. "Don't expect anything," she said.

I wanted to say that I wasn't expecting anything, that it didn't matter what she looked like, but she had already lifted the mirror and was carrying it out of the room.

She took all the mirrors down and piled them like old photographs in the cubbyhole under the stairs. "Why are you doing this?" Father asked when he heard one of the mirrors crack. Mother stopped and looked up at him. You could say she was trying to stare him down, but her eyes were not strong enough to focus. They wavered back and forth — shivering.

Father shifted his weight. "Doreen." He sighed. "How am I going to shave?"

She lifted the stack of mirrors and pulled out a small one that used to hang in my room. I had made it at summer camp by gluing small seashells and colored glass to the rim. They had been washed by the ocean and they were smooth and warm to touch. As she handed it to Father, a periwinkle shell fell off and lay between them. Neither of them reached for the shell so I dipped down quickly and picked it up, white grains of sand dropping like salt on the dark floor.

Father put the mirror under his arm and walked to his room.

Mother looked up at me. "Do you want one, too?"

I studied the inside of the periwinkle shell. It was mauve like the still-bruised parts of Mother's face. "Not now," I said.

We had scrambled eggs and toast for supper. Mother had put a bit of pink lipstick on and it was smudged at the corners of her mouth. Her dark straight hair was pulled back in a tight French braid, a style Father once complimented her on. I searched for something familiar in her face while she told Father her recipe for salmon casserole. Mother didn't cook any more than she had before the accident. Homemade jellies and jams were her specialty. "Things for toast," Father always criticized.

Still, long ago, he had taken us in the lobster boat to Butter Island where wild strawberries grew thick and fragrant on the grassy hillside. Gwen and Mother and Father and I spent hours on the island filling our berry pails in the warm bright sun. At last, Mother lay down in the sweet berries and closed her eyes. Father knelt and kissed her. "I am Butter Island," she announced.

"No one is an island." Father smiled, standing up and sticking a piece of hay at the corner of his mouth. "But if we could be,

I would be Great Spruce Island." He pointed west to a high and wooded island that seemed bigger and stronger than Butter Island but also seemed to match it somehow. Mother stood and held his hand. Father looked down at Gwen and me. "Gwen," he said, pointing north, "you're Beach Island." We both stood and followed his pointing finger. That island was low with a curving beach. "There are thousands of beautiful shells there," he said. "Treasures." He leaned over and picked me up, then looked south. "And you, my little one, you are Fling." Off in the distance, a small island shone yellow in the afternoon sun and on its hilltop lay two green knolls.

"What are those bumps?" I asked.

"Island babies." Father smiled. "Someday, they'll be their own islands."

Even though I was only four, the day wove itself inside me like brightly colored yarn woven into a bird's nest. I loved the oily-smelling boat and the sea breeze in my wild hair and I would come to measure all days by that perfect one. Gwen, too, kept it alive by nicknaming me Fling. Looking at the islands, I imagined them together as one great family before they broke and floated apart.

That day, Gwen and I followed our parents back to the boat. They were holding hands with pails of berries at their sides. Together, they created a beautiful symmetry. Father's broad tanned neck glistened in the sun and Mother's berry-stained blouse billowed behind her, looking like a painting of sea roses.

Soon after, Father sold the lobster boat. I suppose he was already planning to sell it when we boated out for the berries. He was so happy and free that day, even playful, the same way I've heard people behave when they have finalized plans for ending their life. Maybe selling the boat was like that for him. It was a door to his past being closed.

After Mother's accident, she invented recipes and recited them to us at the supper table. Some part of her was finally trying to be the wife Father wanted her to be. She used words like *spin* and *split* and *twirl* to describe the procedures. When she went on too long, Father got agitated. "Please, Doreen, let's just eat what we have before us."

Mother looked down at the eggs that were shaped like a boomerang on her plate. "I'm trying, Peter."

For a moment, there were only our chewing sounds, then Mother said something about the lovely sweetness of wild strawberry preserves. I can't remember exactly what she said, but I know she used the word *essence*. Later, I would look essence up in the dictionary and see it explained as: "the most important feature of a thing that determines its identity."

Father stood up and his chair fell to the

floor. "Why do you always defy me, Doreen?"

"I'm not defying anyone." Mother's eyes were glassy green and bloodshot.

Father pushed his plate from the table. His toast flew almost to the sink, but the plate fell straight down and rumbled on the floor. I don't think he wanted to be angry, but it came over him as naturally as kicking something after you run into it. "Forget it," he said walking off to his room. "Just forget it."

Mother began piling the dirty dishes, eggs and all. There was a lump in my throat and I tried to swallow it down. Mother watched me. "Don't pay any attention to him, Elizabeth. He's hopeless."

Hopeless? I pictured Father driving the lobster boat after his father had been swept overboard, wondering if he kept looking behind, thinking maybe his father would be washed back into the boat in a great wave or if he simply faced forward refusing to hope.

Later, Mother and I pieced together a puzzle of a European castle. The castle was gray and had several huge turrets. Most of the background was dark so I tried to sort the pieces by shade, but Mother said that type of organizing usually turned out to be a waste of time.

"Let her do it her own way," Father said. It was the first he had spoken since supper.

He'd hung my shell mirror by his door and it slanted forward on the wall, reflecting him. He was sitting in a straight-back chair near the center of his room reading a book. Earlier, he'd oohed at something he was reading. In the mirror, his lips were moving with the words. He held his burning cigarette close to his mouth, sucking on it each time he took a new breath.

Mother and I watched Father's reflection. He turned his head slightly and looked down at the floor. The lines on his forehead were shaped like waves and he seemed to be looking for something. Suddenly, Mother grabbed a puzzle piece from my hand and studied it. She slipped it in the lower left corner of the puzzle and smoothed it with her fingers. Her fingernails were cut so short that the pink tips of her fingers stood out as if swelling with heat. I thought about my parents then in a way I never had before, how their shades were visible, but it was hard to figure out where their pieces fit together.

In the spring, a man disappeared and they dragged the lily pond looking for him. We had not been there since the accident. Father and I walked up the road and stood by the shore to watch. The air was fresh and salty. The men lifted and hauled the big net anxiously into their boat, but all they pulled up were deep-rooted weeds and a black mud that shone green in the sun. I was disappointed that a body didn't appear from under the dark water. I thought that the news of a dead man might change my parents or at least change things back to the way they used to be. "Do you think Mother will skate next winter?" I asked.

Father's hand tightened around mine. It was rough and there were small dots of burnt sienna paint along his knuckles. The spring sun was bright, but there was no heat to it. "She doesn't want people to see her," he said.

I fell away then, falling slowly like an overripe berry slipping from its vine. I looked out to the pond as I look out to it now, my eyes frowning. A man stood with his empty net rolled in his arms. In the glare of sunlight, his small boat blended with the water and for a moment he seemed to be the only one on the pond, watching as the springs bled from the earth and made a pool around him. A seagull swooped down and screeched at him and he looked up. His face was shining in the sun the way my mother's always had when she glided on the ice above.

2

Father once told me it was the whiteness of the whale that above all things appalled Ahab. And it is the memory of the slender white bone jutting out between my mother's eyes that pierces me. The sun on white snow is not white enough to compare, nor is the first tooth of a child, nor do I believe will be the cloak of Jesus when I see it.

Sometimes I took the long way to school, going first to the edge of the pond to look for that bone. Many nights I dreamed of finding it cradled in a nautilus shell, but if by chance I'd found it lying there I'm not sure I could have touched it. Like the memory of the last skating night, it had taken on mythical proportions. A whale tucked beneath a pillow. Still, deep in me was that dream to retrieve the bone and put it back where it belonged, just as there was the dream to retrieve my sister, Gwen, and my grandfather at the ocean's bottom and my other deceased grandparents, and my parents' fleeting love for one another, that was as ghostly an image as any departed relative.

One day after walking home from school in

a blizzard, I stepped into the kitchen where the woodstove cracked and snapped. A piece of haddock was simmering on the back of the stove, which told me Father had probably taken fish in trade for a painting.

Father and Mother were in Father's room off the kitchen. Mother was sitting in the straight-back chair in the center of the room. The ceiling light hung on a thin wire directly over her, like the interrogation lighting seen in movies. Bright and unforgiving. Mother's melted-looking face was held proud for Father to study. He kept sweeping in, brushing his fingers over her cheeks and forehead. It seemed he was trying to coax her old face out, as if it were simply hiding. Even with the light beaming down though, Mother's face looked dull. The accident had stolen her expressions and the bright light didn't reflect, but lay flat on her face, making it two dimensional and shadowed like a painting. In its penumbra, I thought I saw defiance, but her emotions lay so deeply behind her masklike face that I could not be sure. This lack of connection with Mother seemed to relax Father, but it cut me adrift like an abandoned dory.

Father concentrated on the easel, his brown eyes held by a serious gaze while he pointed, then slapped his brush on the canvas. He was using gray paint with streaks of white still unmixed on the brush. The gray was the color of a snow goose. "Elizabeth," Mother said, "your father's doing a portrait of me."

"Oh" was all I could say, when what I really wanted to say was, *Why? Why now? When you're no longer beautiful. Why doesn't he stick to his silly boats?* For so long, I'd silently watched things played out between my parents, but now Mother was at a disadvantage. I wanted to defend her, but I was afraid of Father's temper, so I stood watching her shamefully and quietly. Years later, I read the words of Marguerite Duras, who described her own aging face as "ravaged." It made me stop and try to think of a word to describe Mother's face after the accident. Melted, as if she was disappearing before my very eyes? Mangled, as if long-ago Eskimo dogs had chewed upon her face? But in the end, Duras's word seemed to suit Mother, too. Ravaged. Maybe in the end, it suits all women.

That day Mother was wearing white tights and a red skating skirt with a matching sweater. The blades had been removed from her skates. "Mother, what happened to your skates?"

She turned slightly, her neck seeming stiff. "I had your father unscrew the blades."

Suddenly, the small red mitten trapped in the ice at the pond came back to me and I wanted to be trapped with it. Sealed like a lily under glass. The blizzard that had been rattling the windows seeped through the house and I raised my voice to speak. Firmly, I asked, "Why did you have him take the blades off?"

"Because I want to wear the boots. They feel good on my feet." Mother relaxed her neck and looked back to Father. "Don't paint me as a freak," she said teasingly.

"Doreen, don't be foolish." Father's eyes were made up of all the primary colors, muddled and brown.

"Well, that's what I am," she said.

My eyes dropped to her legs that were strong and sinewy under her white tights. I pictured myself clinging to her neck while she skated on the pond. White legs on white ice, my body flying, my face nestled in the softness of her neck. The image was so beautiful as to make me hear music, a piano being played on the high and youthful black keys — the ones that children always choose to play. It was encompassing until Father brought me back — "Elizabeth" — his voice hitting the region of the lower more serious keys. "Your boots are getting the floor wet, Elizabeth."

Behind the woodstove, I took my boots off. Only then did I realize that my face had been frozen while walking home from school. It tingled and ached. I hung my jacket and ski pants behind the stove, then sat on the tiny bench against the wall. It was a bench made of rough and uneven wood and we considered it Father's. In the summer, he took it into the grove of scrub pine at the side of our yard to sit and smoke. Once, he started a small fire by tossing a burning cigarette into the dried needles. Mother and I watched from the window as Father crazily put the fire out, lifting his legs high and stomping. It was as wild and free as I'd ever seen him. Maybe a crisis is what frees people. Maybe we spend our entire lives avoiding what we should embrace.

I stood up and took my skates from the hook. They had not been touched since the accident. The leather around the ankles was stiff while I knew the boots of Mother's skates to be warm and wrinkled. Rubbing the creases, I could always touch her years of practice and dedication. And I could feel the happiness skating brought because the wrinkles were shaped like gentle smiles.

I imagined slipping my skates on, tightening the laces and hearing the blades tap and pound against the ice. "T's," I heard Mother say, "make T pushoffs."

I stepped around to the front of the stove and took the lid off, then stuffed my skates into the fire. They blackened quickly, smothering the air. When they were seared and black, I stuffed Gwen's skates in on top of mine and watched them burn together. After Mother's accident, I'd asked if Gwen could

40

come back home, but Father only stared at me. "Why?" I pleaded. "Why can't she be part of this family?"

It was inconceivable to me that she had been so quickly snipped from the portrait of us. "Why?" I asked again and again.

"Because she wouldn't listen," he finally said.

"She listened, Dad, she just didn't . . ." I wanted to go on, but Father was watching my lips as if each word weighed as heavy as an anchor.

Gwen used to lie next to me in her twin bed, telling me what it felt like to be with her Italian boyfriend. She used the word *smooth*, which I didn't understand. "Where do you do *it*?" I asked.

"Under the steps of the Opera House."

I pictured the big gray shiplike building at the other end of the village. Sometimes, in the summer, a play would run there or a concert, but mostly it was left empty. Long grass and cobwebs grew under the rickety steps. "Isn't it creepy under there?"

"No." Gwen breathed. "Tony brings a blanket. No one can see us, we're hidden, but we can hear everything."

"Hear what?"

"People passing on the gravel beside us, music from the legion hall, the hum of the quarry, kids crying, dogs barking . . . You know. Village sounds. It's cozy."

While Father and I finished eating our haddock in cream, Mother pushed her plate of uneaten dinner to the center of the table and began to draw with a pencil. "Don't you like your dinner?" Father asked.

"I'm afraid of getting a bone," she said. The word *bone* echoed from the hollow of her lips. Bone. White and pointed bone, rumbling on the table of our memories.

Mother drew ruffled circles on white paper, a series overlapping within an oblong shape, the clouds of warmer weather and thunderstorms. If Father had painted them, he probably would have used the same gray he'd used earlier to portray Mother's face.

Someone knocked on the door and Mother stood up quickly. She faced the door, dropping her glance to check our faces. We must have revealed shame, because she turned quickly, trying to push off with her amputated skates. Finally, she took an awkward step, and another, but before she had reached the sink, the door opened and the blizzard blew coldly and forcefully into the kitchen.

"Lochard," Father said, standing to shake hands. His son stepped in behind him. His black wool hat was pulled down tightly around his head and his face was blotched red from the cold. They both wore green rubber boots, the ones they wore out to sea to gather lobsters. "Come in," Father said.

I could never look at Michael MacDonald, who was two years older than me, without picturing his mother, Bertie. She was a good friend of my mother's. Big warm-voiced Bertie, her strong Stonington accent breaking the syllables of dear in two, as softly as a warm cookie: *De'ah, de'ah, my de'ah.* Bertie was missing two fingers on her right hand: the middle and the index. Some said they'd been cut off accidentally while she worked at the sardine plant when she was young. Julie Ann Sparrow said Mr. MacDonald chopped them off because she played the piano in their living room too often. That didn't seem possible. He was a gentle man. Besides, the space where Bertie's fingers should have been echoed something different, something as faint as children's voices echoing up from the shore.

Mother was standing at the sink with a square white cloth over her head. She must have rummaged through the dishcloth drawer for something to hide her face. How strange she must have looked to the visitors in full skating attire with a red-stained cloth over her face. It was the cheesecloth she always used to make cranberry jelly in the fall. She'd tie it up to make a bag for the boiled cranberries and hook it on the cupboard handle where blood-colored juice dripped through into the silver bowl below. Like the burning skates, the cranberries would leave a bitter smell in the house for days.

Mother stepped forward gently like a bride from a place of strange customs. A bride of freaks, you might say. She finally seemed to have control over her amputated boots and her walk was graceful. Remembering it, I think of it as grace-filled. She reached her hand to Mr. MacDonald, then to Michael. "The light is still very hard on my eyes," she said, "I have to keep my face covered."

Mr. MacDonald's chest seemed to sink. "We won't keep you," he said. "Michael has something to say."

Michael stepped into the light of the kitchen. He'd taken his hat off and unzipped his coat. A white tooth hung on a black cord around his neck. Probably a shark's tooth. It was shaped like the bone that had broken through Mother's head. "I'm sorry," he said, breaking down like a boy who had been caught stealing. "I should have looked before I shot the puck." Michael hiccupped and gasped for air. His black hair hung in a pile over one eye.

Mother touched his shoulder. Her hand lay as white as snow on his navy pea coat. "Michael, didn't you used to help me do my spirals?"

He looked up, wiping his nose with the back of his hand, "Yes, ma'm."

Mother often coaxed a boy from a game of hockey to hold her hands while she circled around him stretching backward over the ice, her face tilted upward and her head almost touching the frozen surface, a perfect death spiral.

"Doing those were some of the happiest times of my life," she said, excusing herself to go upstairs, unsteady like a drunken woman, one who always leaves the bar late, but chooses to be alone.

For burning up the skates, Father only scolded me. He said if I really wanted to destroy them I should have thought of a better way. I hated him in that moment. His desire to simply erase bad situations seemed unforgivable. Earlier, Father had pulled my scorched skates from the stove and put them in the trash. Of course I wanted him to make a fuss, telling me I'd have to skate every day for the rest of my life, then screwing mother's blades back on her skates for me to use. But he simply knotted the trash bag and took it out to the shed.

Mother had been in bed for hours when Father and I sat down at the table to eat a bowl of cereal. Her cloud drawing lay between us. "Do you believe in ghosts?" I asked.

"Only as a remote possibility," he said.

I wasn't sure what he meant so I said, "What about phantoms?"

Father lifted his cereal bowl and drank the milk in the bottom. His hands looked too big for the bowl: a man's hands around the neck of a swan.

"What about phantoms?" I asked again.

He put the bowl down. "Only in paintings," he said, dismissing the conversation to talk about the warming weather and smoke a cigarette.

After, I looked at the painting on his easel. I was hoping for Mother as she used to look, but instead it was Mother's damaged face. He'd used the gray paint to give a transparent effect. On her flat forehead he had drawn a miniature skating scene, much like the one we'd all been part of the last night of skating. *Ghost as a remote possibility, as in ghost of chance.* I thought of the tooth around Michael's neck. Maybe it was the bone from Mother's face. I imagined snatching it and running home with it held between my teeth like a dog with a bone, but even in this fantasy, my ankles felt shackled.

When Gwen and I were little and the moon was full, Father would drive us out over the great Deer Isle bridge to an apple orchard in Brooklin. Mother and Gwen and I loved the high green suspension bridge that connected Little Deer Isle to the mainland.

Beneath us, sailboats floated as if in a dream and the azure sky seemed close enough to touch. Going over the bridge was like traveling over the back of a great dragon and every time the car glided onto the mainland side, we all sighed as if we'd been holding our breath for a very long time. Mother always took a box of Ganong chocolates with her, eating them like popcorn. Her Canadian girlfriend Cheryl worked at the Ganong factory in St. Stephen and constantly mailed freebies to Mother. As a result, Gwen and I tired of them at a young age. Occasionally, Mother would hold the box up over the seat toward us and Gwen would say, "Yuck, *Gag Ons.*" Mother would smile, popping another one in her mouth and savoring it as if she were tasting her homeland.

One night, at the side of the road near the Brooklin apple orchard, we watched the moonlight dally in the branches. Beyond, you could see the shimmering water of Eggemoggin Reach. Like a hundred times before, Father would tell us of a house that used to sit behind the orchard. It belonged to a lady whose husband had been lost at sea. When she was living and when the moon was full, Father said she called out for her husband. Often, people passing by heard her calling and walked into the orchard to investigate. Father said the branches of the trees came down, grabbed the intruders, and strangled them. "Why?" Gwen always asked, making a face behind Father.

Father would suck hard on his cigarette, then blow the smoke out toward the dark and shadowy orchard. "Because they had no business being there."

Gwen rolled her eyes. Neither of us could have put it into words, but we knew Father was threatening us with our own deaths. If we dared to venture out, something terrible would befall us. Somehow he'd already managed to make ghosts of us, hanging our girl skeletons in the apple orchard. We were to stay in Stonington, at the other side of the great bridge where we belonged. We were to take no highways. His fear or jealousy of the world, as Mother always called it, made me feel as lightweight as a cobweb blowing under the Opera House steps. Clearly, the world could blow me away if it wanted to. The only way to protect myself was to hide.

"Now," he'd say, starting the car, "let's go on up the road and get ourselves some ice cream." That was our reward for listening. Off we'd go, the car sweet with the smell of chocolate and the crickets bleating like babies in the night fields around us.

Outside my bedroom window, snow was coming down in splinter-shaped needles. First, snow shaped like miniature trees came and clung to the windowpane. I'd seen the same shapes in stones by the sea and later I would learn that they were called dendrites. As the frost and ice melted from the center of the window, the crystals grew longer like blades from tiny skates.

That night, I dreamed of babies skating in long white gowns. Hundreds of them, cooing and gliding and twirling.

By morning, an icicle had grown into a long dagger outside my window. In the sunlight, it reflected like crystal. I pried the window open and reached to bring the icicle in, but it broke and fell like a sword into the snow below. I wanted to take it to Mother. I thought if she touched the thing that used to free her, she might be healed. Instead, I nervously ate the cold piece that broke into my hand, making my head throb and my teeth ache.

Later, I looked for Michael MacDonald in the school corridor, because I didn't want any more surprise visitors. When I found him, he hung his head as if to hide the shark's tooth with his chin. "Do you think my mother's a freak?" I asked.

"Of course not."

"Well, she is," I told him, "so it's best you not come around."

"Elizabeth," he said coming after me. I turned and looked into his eyes, which were somehow caressing.

"It's not like a couple of missing fingers, de'ah," I mocked.

After, I cried in the girls' bathroom, sitting crowded beside the cold white toilet with my face buried in my hands. My cheeks were dry from windburn and felt as if they were peeling away. What if something happened to my face, I thought, would I not want mirrors? Would I sit at the table and draw mammatus clouds? Would I hide my strange face from the faces of strangers? I wanted to run until I reached the harbor. In that time of frozen land and whipping winds, I knew the sea would be moving, in and out as if breathing, but I stayed where I was, surrounded by tiles as cold and candescent as the skin of a beached whale.

3

Above all else, Father was an aesthete. After Mother's accident, her beauty, which had satisfied him for so long, was suddenly gone, and that seemed to free him from the lifeless fishing boats. He painted in a frenzy, raging colorful paintings that he began to sell at one of the galleries in Blue Hill. His completed canvasses were no longer two dimensional. Instead, they breathed fire, as if he had allowed himself to escape to the mainland and was looking back into the mouth of the dragon bridge.

Mother moved deeper into the house and it was often hard to find her. It was as if she'd sunk into its layers and was somehow hidden behind the walls. Months later I would learn that she'd been in the cubbyhole under the stairs. With the mirrors.

An art dealer from Boston named Celise came on a rainy spring day and stayed into the evening drinking scotch with Father. The air was both fresh and sour with birth as if beneath the primula an ancient fetid river flowed. While Celise tried to convince Father of his painting talent, he told her stories of lobstering, unfamiliar stories about gallant rescues, surprise storms and Grand Bank catches. The more Celise wanted Father to look at his future, the more he seemed to look back, but finally with Celise's light touches to his hand and her welcoming laugh (a throwing of the head, revealing her slim white throat and a plush open mouth), Father gave in and was soon drunk with dreams.

I don't believe Celise thought I had a mother, because whenever I came into the kitchen, she complimented me on the house as if it were my charge. She stretched out some of her words like lazy snakes basking in the sun: "And I just *love* that saying on the *plaque* by the door."

> *You don't have to thank us or laugh*
> *at our jokes,*
> *Sit deep and come often, you're one of*
> *the folks.*

"Isn't that the cutest *saying?*" she cooed.

I wanted to tell her the *plaque* was a wedding present to my *parents*, but before I could say anything, the words evaporated in my throat, dried by Celise's breezy way.

She left that evening with two paintings under her arm. Father watched until her car was out of sight.

"Mother hasn't had her supper," I scolded.

He gave me a quizzical look. "Well, take her something."

"I can't find her," I screamed.

Father went into his painting room and picked up his book, opened it and looked back at me. He looked slightly afraid. "I need to think," he said. I believe he was contemplating disloyalty. I know now there is a look about it. A scurrying of the eyes.

The following day, Mother had a followup appointment at the hospital in Bangor, so we all went along. It would be her last by choice. The doctor suggested small things she could do with makeup to lessen the effect of the injury, and in what seemed like an afterthought, he suggested she talk to one of the hospital's therapists. Mother was sitting very straight in a chair, the same way she had sat for Father to paint her. Maybe she saw herself as a study. If she did, she was brave about it, her chin slightly lifted toward the doctor. I'd read once that a dying whale will turn and face the sun and I saw Mother dying over and over while these men passed judgment, the warmth they shed on her as minimal and distant as the heat from a winter sun. "I'll be fine without a therapist." She smiled.

On our way home, Mother lay across the backseat. It was the way she traveled. Hidden. Tucked like a penny in a child's hand. People we passed saw it as Father and me driving together, but I knew Mother would be ever present no matter where she hid. Omnipresent, Only, the echoing O of that icy opaque.

We stopped at the Co-Op for some lobsters. I couldn't help but think of the lily pond on up the road. The white and pink lilies would be sleeping now as Mother, facing the hot backseat, slept behind us.

Father wanted female lobsters because he enjoyed eating the roe, so I helped pick them from the tank, turning each one over to find the soft feathery feelers. The male feelers were hard and shaped like a pointing finger.

Lochard MacDonald was manning the wharf and he asked how Mother was doing. "Fine," I said, studying his face, imagining it as the sea and his wrinkles as the routes he'd taken to find the lobsters. Someday his son, Michael, would take the same routes. This was the course of many Stonington boys, or maybe better to say the curse. What loving woman would ever wish it for her husband or son? Father had warned me many times that the sea was possessed by its own moods and spirit, and men and women were almost nothing to it. So that I, too, began to fear.

One night, during a particularly lean winter, just after my Canadian grandparents were killed in a car crash, Mother suggested we all move to Pennfield Ridge, New Brunswick. She said her family's house was just sitting there, empty. "Peter," she continued, "you could get a good paying job at the paper mill and still do your painting."

Father had been languid on the kitchen couch, chewing tobacco and reading, but he stopped everything abruptly, glaring over his book with the broken spine. He rolled the juicy tobacco between his lips, and corralled it to his cheek. "Why would I want to go there?"

Gwen and I were doing our homework at the table. Mother came and stood between us, putting a hand on each of our shoulders as if she was already leading us somewhere new. "For them," she said. "There's no life for them here."

Father sat up, gathering his tobacco near his lips, spitting it into the old coffee can beside him. He wiped a streak of dark spit from his chin. "Stop putting ideas in their heads, Doreen. This *is* their life. Besides, Pennfield Ridge isn't any different from here."

"Pennfield Ridge," Mother said, "has a highway running through it. You can get on that road and you can end up some place."

"Your parents were killed on that highway, Doreen. I wouldn't get all romantic about it." Father got up and went into his painting room, slamming the door. We all looked at one another. Mother moved to the window, into her own widow's walk, watching, waiting, hoping. While still staring out, she said, "You girls make sure you marry someone kind, so it won't matter where you live."

When Father and I returned to the car with the lobsters, Mother had curled up and was shaking. "Are you all right?" I asked, reaching over the seat. Mother ignored my hand as if drifting on a cold sea, shaking from hours of being lost. Father opened the back door and put the bag of lobsters on the floor. They moved and clacked in the bag. He touched Mother's head to steady her. "It's okay, Doreen, we're going right home."

Of course, neither of us knew Mother was having a seizure and that this would be the first of many. The radio was on low, *Only the lonely:* that *only* and *lonely* so sweetly and shallowly, shakingly sung.

Even with the windows down, the glaring sun made the car feel like a pressure cooker. Chewing my bottom lip, I tried to spot buoys on the sea as we drove off, but my teary eyes blurred the sea and I couldn't envision an anchor.

Before we came to a complete stop in the driveway, Mother was out of the car, staggering toward the house. Inside, we found her at the sink mixing what looked like flour and water. Neither Father nor I went near her. Something about her had changed, something far greater than beauty into bloated ugliness, something more powerful. Father and I stood motionless while she gathered the bowl into her arms and walked away, milky water sloshing down her still-strong legs.

Later, Father boiled the lobsters and I spread newspapers on the kitchen table. Mother had taken a bath and her hair hung like dark ferns around her face. Her face was so white that I wondered if she'd used the flour mixture as a face pack before bathing. There were small cuts on her fingers that I hadn't noticed earlier, as if she'd spent the day cracking and opening many hard-shelled lobsters. One of her hands was still shaking.

Mother and I only ate the lobster claws and tails, leaving the remains for Father. With each one, he pulled the legs off one by one, drawing the meat out between his teeth. Then, he went for the body, splitting it with his hands and pecking out the shreds of meat before savoring the tomalley.

"How can you eat that stuff?" Mother asked.

"It's ambrosia," he said.

Father had never used that word before. It was a city word, a Celise word, a word of cupidity, but then as if he realized that himself, he cleared his throat and said he'd been brought up on lobsters. They were as natural to him as milk to a baby. It was also strange that he mentioned milk in the same breath as lobster, since he often said the combination of the two would make you violently ill. "That's not true," Mother always said. "What about lobster stew?" Still, neither Gwen nor I dared to experiment, any more than we would have dared to walk through the haunted apple orchard in Brooklin.

After dark, Mother often went out of the house. She would rush to the lily pond and walk around it in a navy wool pea coat, the hood pulled up to hide her shattered face. Years later the locals would still reminisce about the ghost of Doreen Johnson, and Julie Ann Sparrow would delight in telling me how the teenagers dared one another to run and touch her, but to my knowledge, no one ever did. Once, Father tried to catch Mother and bring her back home, but she resisted by punching him hard between the eyes.

When Celise returned weeks later with a large check for Father's paintings and a bottle of Dewar's, the bruise was still there, looking as round and cool as a quarter. Celise touched it and said, "Oooh." I was at the kitchen table rubbing Noxzema into my sunburnt arms and the seducing cool of Celise's *ooh* matched the smell of menthol and eucalyptus.

There was a hot humid breeze and earlier I had lowered the windows to keep things from blowing around. I returned nothing when Celise smiled at me. Try this for cool, I thought. Her face was heart-shaped and framed by clipped blonde hair. Beside her face, Mother's would be that of a beast. What the accident had taken away from Mother in the way of beauty, though, it paid back with intuition. We always knew when someone was going to knock on our door because Mother disappeared, just as she had that day. Even Father seemed to realize this connection and had washed his face and wet his brush cut, as if hoping for Celise.

"You're going to be a very rich man," Celise said, waving the check near his lips. "Just keep painting."

From my bedroom window, the clouds were large and floating on a rapid invisible current. I wanted to float off with them. It seemed I was always standing at my window with some dilemma washing over me. I wanted to tell my mother about Celise, but I knew it would cause a fight. Once when Mother and Father fought hard and I cried, Mother comforted me by saying Father was a jealous man.

"In what way is he jealous?" I asked.

"Jealous of the world, Elizabeth."

"Why?"

"It changes us," she said matter-of-factly. "To him, it's poison."

Why then had he let the world into our house? Surely, Celise's smiling sounds were a poison.

On my way downstairs, I noticed the cubbyhole door under the stairway slightly ajar. I opened it to find Mother. She'd removed all the mirrors from their frames and laid them on the floor like ice. She was on her knees shaping a pile of white mud when she noticed me. It was stifling under the stairs and Mother's face was bluish and bloated. "Quick," she said, "come in. I don't want your father to know."

I thought the mirrors might crack when I stepped on them, but instead they felt cool and strong. I knelt down, realizing that the white mound was the flour mixture she had mixed the day we returned from the hospital.

"I'm sculpting," she said.

"But, Mother, it's so hot in here, you'll die."

"Oh no," she said.

She smelled sweaty and sour, bordering on rancidity.

"I can't breathe," I said gasping and opening the door to escape. Of course, I'll never know if it was the heat or smell that took my breath away, or if perhaps it was the sight of Mother having found yet another thing to take her away from me.

The quart of scotch and two glasses were on the kitchen table, but Father and Celise had gone into the painting room. Father's paint brushes were gently slapping. Celise sighed with the heat. I tiptoed closer and peeked in. Celise had unbuttoned her blouse and let it drop off her shoulders revealing a gentle cleavage. I pictured an invisible pulley between Father and Celise that would snap if it were not allowed to bring them together. Still, only when I was older would I fully understand how consuming it must have been for them. My strong Father, smoking and squinting, slapping the brushes and she, more than willing to be his muse. I thought of the one portrait he'd done of me. So grown as to never be young, my eyes shamefully lowered. No, not shamefully, nor pensively, not even demurely. Deferentially. Father had painted me the way he wanted me. It was not a portrait, but a wish. *How would he paint Celise?*

I rushed to the cubbyhole. "Mother," I said, "Celise is here."

"I know," she said.

"She's sitting naked for Father to paint her."

Mother touched her floured hand to her face, then got up and walked through the kitchen to the painting room. She was wearing one of Father's shirts and it was covered in dry white plaster as if she were a sculpture, coming to life. She stopped in the doorway.

"Doreen," Father said sternly, "get away."

Celise's chair tumbled over as she rushed to get away from Mother. No doubt the vision of some frightening tale, some piece of folklore that had survived for many years and finally come to life.

Celise's blouse slid to the floor and her slender arms crossed over her chest; *X marks the spot of poison*. Now it was on my father's shores, traveling up one of the very tributaries that led to him. She on one tributary, Mother on another, Gwen on yet another and so on and so on, each stream divided by green forest and strangling underbrush. Whenever we, his girls, tried to join up and come to him as a river, he pushed us back. *Damned us.*

"Doreen." Father moved toward Mother, grabbing her forearm. "Go."

Mother stood firmly, staring at him. Her face was mauve and all her features had softened like clay. She made a fist with the hand that trembled.

Father looked at it quizzically. "What do you want?"

Blue veins raised up on Mother's white neck as if she were being strangled. "I want impunity," she said weakly.

I didn't know what the word meant, but

Father seemed to understand immediately. His mouth dropped as did his eyes, searching the floor like a man who had lost the key to the cage he'd accidentally locked himself in.

Mother left and I followed her partway to the cubbyhole, stopping in the hallway to listen while Father explained things to Celise, then appeased her by offering a painting to sell. It was the painting of Mother with the skating scene on her forehead.

Of course, it would not be the end of Celise. The episode only seemed to increase her desire to visit. Some feed off the passion of others and can hang on tighter than barnacles to the hull of a ship.

Upstairs, the hot summer wind ripped through the windows. The quarry was roaring on Crotch Island and a huge barge passed offshore, its engine muffled by the wind and drilling, its lights glowing gold and lonely. In my mind, Father needed to repent, but I don't think that was what he believed, and as far as I knew there was no synonym for the word. Looking back, I realize he was already painting over the memory of us.

4

The next morning, there was a steady thumping coming from my parents' room. I rushed to their door. Mother was leaning naked over the footboard of their bed and Father was behind her, his broad buttocks much more muscular than I would have imagined. I don't know what their habits of lovemaking were. Outside of an occasional bedspring squeaking in the middle of the night, I had no evidence of their sexual life together. This was my first witnessing. And had I seen it before Mother's face was destroyed, I might not have been so shocked, but the idea of Father holding her down, her face neatly tucked to her chest like an ibis, was shameful to me. I wondered if Father was imagining Celise. Either her or my once beautiful mother, but he was not with the new woman, her features dissolving with each passing day like sand art being swept away by the incoming tide. He was loving too hard and too fast for an injured person.

When he finished, Mother's hands stretched across the footboard and her head hung down. She looked trapped in a guillotine. Father fell down over her. His body looked laden with remorse. Under his weight, Mother must have felt that he'd never allow her to be without punishment, or maybe that was what I was feeling. The accident seemed to have woven a net around all of us, and it was sometimes hard to tell whose feelings belonged to whom. We'd been dumped together like hundreds of shimmering sardines in the bottom of a boat, reflecting one another.

The sky can reflect one's heart, too. That afternoon a fierce wind ripped through, starting with a long thin dust cloud from ground to sky that Father called a dust devil. He said he had only seen one other dust devil and it was the day before he and his father had gone to sea for the last time. It surprised me to hear him mention his father. I feared then something dark might be pending: a clearing of the decks before a brutal storm.

While the windowpanes rattled and rain slashed against the glass, I went to Mother's room and looked through her things. In her night table, under a row of unmatched black buttons, there was a pamphlet describing her medical condition. The definition for her injury was hypertelecanthus, or frontal lobism. The pamphlet said the frontal lobes influence two behavioral functions: learned motor behavior and the planning and organizing of future expressive behavior. I wondered what the organizing of future expressive behavior meant. Was this why Mother was sculpting? Was she grasping at something because she knew it was about to leave her? And was Father doing the same thing with his frantic painting? It occurred to me then that they might love one another deeply, and for some reason, that weighed more heavily on me than all their arguing or violent lovemaking. I imagined them sharing an ancient glass buoy, carelessly tossing it back and forth while each fully understood its irreplaceable value.

Once I found a battered doll on the shore. The doll's brown hair had been chopped short and one foot was missing. Her damaged forehead was cracked and hollow. I loved her because of her possibilities, not the future ones, but her earlier possibilities, the ones I would never know, because she was beyond repair. Her eyes no longer closed when you laid her down. Instead, she stared straight up like a dead child angel gazing. Often just before death, a person's eyes will open wide and stare intently, unhurriedly, with perfect calm, lucid and impenetrable. I thought of the doll as being on the edge of heaven and by loving her, maybe I would be on the edge of something wonderful, too. Father was embarrassed by the doll. He said people would think that he didn't have enough money to buy me a decent doll. "She has decent dolls," Mother said, "but she likes this one."

"That one is damaged," he said, annoyed. Imperfections nagged at him. Just days before, Father had tried to help me draw our house for a school project and became so frustrated with my lack of perspective that he grabbed the paper and finished the drawing himself. After he angrily drew our home, Mother took me to the pond to skate. On the way, she pointed to a small empty house. "A poet by the name of Elizabeth Bishop used to summer in that house. She was a free spirit, raised in Canada." I stared at the empty windows and at the roof, which was caving in. "I named you after her," Mother said, "so there's no reason you can't be a free spirit, too."

There were tears in Mother's eyes. "Dream," she said, patting my cheek with her mitten. "You have to, Elizabeth."

It would only be a matter of days before Mother's head and face began to swell at such a steady rate that we would have to take her to the hospital where the doctor drilled holes in her head to relieve the pressure, the same type of drill that one might use to build a house or a swingset for a child. It seemed wrong that a tool for wood or stone would be used on my mother's head, but again things no longer seemed congruous.

We left Mother late that night in her white room at the hospital. Father watched her from a distance, his face drawn. Mother was asleep and her head was bandaged, but the blood seeped through and made blotches of red around her head. I thought of Christ with thorns pressing, of innocence betrayed, wondering if that might be the definition of marriage.

When Father and I got home from the hospital, the sun was just coming up. The warm wind was still blowing, but its rage was gone. It was now a breeze. Something warm and welcoming. Something to behold. The sun, which had been missing for days, had broken through low in the sky. It cast the harbor in a glorious pink, pink as overwhelming sadness, the same sadness Jacqueline Kennedy must have felt looking at her husband's Sherwood Pink gravestone. Life could turn so quickly. We'd been shaped by a night of skating. *Pink sky at night, sailor's delight. Pink sky in the morning, sailor take warning.*

The pink morning sky gradually became orange, then reddened, as if beneath the horizon something was burning. Mother once told me about a phoenix setting fire to itself so as to rise anew from its ashes. Could such a thing happen? Could we make something of our own ashes?

When I went downstairs, Father was sitting at the table, smoking. "I've asked her back," he said.

I'd already prepared a little speech on Celise. "You asked who back?" I said angrily.

"Your sister, Gwen." Her name was as wispy as the cigarette smoke coming from his mouth.

"But you don't like her," I said.

Father stared at me, his dark eyes narrowing. "Like has nothing to do with it."

I looked up at the ceiling where rain had left stains in the shape of the granite islands of Merchants Row. Tears came down my face. Father reached to touch them, but I pushed his hand away, hating him, but hating my tears more. He stood up and took me in his arms. Buried there, I could smell the salty sea and something of his own smell, which was like pine boughs. I wanted more than anything to stay there forever, nestled in the bed of him.

A week later, Gwen had still not arrived home, but Mother was home from the hospital and Father had packed his things and left. He did this in the night without us knowing. In the morning, a note lay on the kitchen table, weighed down by nothing. *I'll call you.*

While I fixed a breakfast tray of toast and

tea for Mother, I wondered how I'd tell her. Only days earlier, the doctor said a calm and organized environment was what she needed. She was having more seizures and memory lapses where she remembered very little of her life, including my name. Each trip to the hospital deprived her of something. Not only was her left arm shaking and her mood solemn, but now saliva leaked from her lips. She constantly used tissues to wipe it away and they lay crumpled on her bedroom floor like withered lilies. Often she stared down at them, bewildered, her emerald eyes as translucent as bubbling springs. Then she'd tell me something of our family's history. At the time, I didn't know if her stories were imagined or real, but they held me closely to her, closer than I had ever been. She told me how Grandfather Johnson brought my French grandmother to Stonington after the war. How they had two children, then parted, my grandmother making the long trip back to France with Father's younger sister, Marie, and Father staying behind.

"How cruel," I said.

Mother looked at me. "It was all she could do, Elizabeth. She was so homesick for Calais."

"But she left one of her children behind."

"Yes." Mother nodded. "Your father always said he and his sister were divided up like candy, but Marie came back when she was older." Mother looked to the window, stretching her neck as if she had caught sight of something flying by. Her eyes were clear, yet soft looking. She smiled. When I looked with her, there was nothing to see, but the blue, blue heavens.

I know now the damaged are capable of seeing things we cannot. A clairvoyance washes over them. Ask anyone who has an injured loved one. At times, their eyes open like hinged shells revealing a mysteriously moist and pulsating world.

Before Mother's tea had steeped, the telephone rang. I took a deep breath, trying to think of what to say to Father, then answered.

There was a pause.

"Hey, Fling." Gwen's voice was sweeter and lusher, a bird's song coming from a covert of limbs and greenery. "How are you?"

"I'm okay. Where are you?"

"I'm at Aunt Marie's," she said.

"When are you coming home?"

Gwen was quiet. There was a static coastal forecast on a radio in the background, but I couldn't make it out. I looked out at the harbor. The water had never sparkled more. "Fling," she said, "I can't."

"Why not? Father wants you to. He wants you back here." I couldn't admit to her that he was gone. I hadn't yet admitted it to myself. Besides, wasn't that the thing we were all looking for? Father's love.

She laughed nervously.

"He does," I said. "Why can't you come?"

She said she had a job waitressing and might even be getting married. I pictured her that way, married, and tears came in my throat. Even though I could not have said it then, marriage seemed a slow bleed for women, similar to the slow bleed that would eventually betray and silently kill our mother.

"Why can't you come back, Gwen?"

"I'm afraid," she said flatly. "I can't come back now."

"What are you afraid of? Are you afraid of Father?"

"I'm afraid of a lot of things."

"Like what?"

"Like getting trapped there."

I felt hot and lifted the window, cradling the telephone receiver beneath my chin. The air was oily and smelled of fish remains. A fish rots from the head, the locals always said when they were frustrated with the unfair powers of others being forced upon them. That perfect day when Father took us strawberry picking on Butter Island came like a breeze. *No one is an island,* he'd declared, but we were all islands; some weathering the days better than others and some beauties sinking, because of what came their way.

"Hang on a second, Gwen." I sat on the floor and laid the telephone receiver beside me. Should I say something of what Mother told me a few nights ago: the Italian baby that Gwen carried. Father taking her to a so-called doctor in Bangor, a second-storey walkup with a garlicky smelling entrance, and a back windowless room where two wooden pegs were placed in Gwen's uterus, before she was returned home. The next day, after much cramping, the Italian baby lay in the toilet water, no more than a spittle of red and clotted blood, the wooden pegs like a broken bough beneath a new bird, lost in a fall from its nest. Mother said Gwen sat in her bed and cried, sometimes humming "Rock-a-Bye, Baby," and sometimes rocking herself. There was no consoling her. She bled so heavily as to finally lie faint in the bed, at which time Mother ordered Father to take her to the hospital, where she was treated and told she'd never be able to have children. What did Father say to Gwen on the way to hospital? Did he tell her a story of someone else's demise? Was I to become like Father? Trapping someone I love with a haunting rendering from the past?

I looked down at the receiver, its black shape morbidly fetal, then picked it up and cupped it to the side of my face. "Gwen? Guess what?"

"What?"

"Mother says our grandfather didn't drown by accident."

I waited for her reply in the hollow tunnel silence that only telephone conversations can provide. "Did you hear me, Gwen?"

"Yes," she said solemnly. "Is Mother telling family secrets?"

"I guess so."

There was a moment, a still and silent moment, as if Gwen were waiting for a dark cloud to pass, then a faint "bye" and the line clicked, leaving a heavy silence, heavier than all Father's threatening stories ever cast upon me.

In a few weeks, the slow bleed had taken Mother. I found her lying in her bed, staring straight up with perfect calm: the battered doll. One emerald eye was glassy, yet warm looking, while the other eye was bloodshot with a pink tear dried beneath it. Her lips were parted, making me believe she died while calling someone's name.

I touched her white swan neck, which was as warm and soft as feathers. Death had its own life, its own blanket of stillness. Mother's eyes were like windows that had been opened to let the sea-blue heaven in. Their gaze was both shallow and endless, but somehow void of any reflection.

I leaned in and kissed her cheek, then licked the dry tear, which tasted of bitter cranberries. It seemed she came around me then, filling the room like a beam of warm light.

I imagined for the shortest second that she was on her way back to me, that she had only slipped into death for a moment. I had read about loved ones returning, but Mother's eyes simply kept their still and steady concentration. They reflected nothing of my wishes.

Several times, I attempted to close her eyes. I'd seen it done in movies many times, but I couldn't bring myself to do it. It seemed so final, but in the end, I was able to close them by remembering her skating, smooth strong strokes, strong and spirited enough to carry us both. Closing them was as easy as silking down the feathers of an infant bird.

I lay my head over her heart. Her chest was solid and had turned as cool and quiet as a cellar and already she smelled of musty earth.

Later I caught myself standing at Mother's window, flapping my hands as if they were on fire, calling for her. She still lay in her bed and I wanted her to get up and walk, to skate again, to tell me things, to say, *Dream, Elizabeth, dream.* This was too real. It was as fresh as a wide cut slashed across my chest, but bleeding inside instead of out, hemorrhaging.

Too soon, a large seabird passed by Mother's window. I turned to see a quick gliding shadow sweep over her and I knew she had made her escape. All other departures were mere child's play.

5

After Mother was buried, Julie Ann Sparrow's father brought me a black-faced Eskimo dog for company. He handed me the red leash and said, "Dogs hold the souls of the dead, Elizabeth. Especially the females."

Her arrival was bittersweet, reminding me of our dog, Sadie, whom Father shot for disobeying him. The new dog had the very eyes of Sadie, blue and pleading forgiveness, even though no obvious sin had been committed.

I called her Sheila, a name that seemed warm but somehow like ice, a name I would have liked for myself. It was late September and Sheila's gray coat was thickening. Just after arriving, she went into heat. At first, it frightened me. Blood had never been a good sign, but then Julie Ann Sparrow explained it. "She's just ready for babies, Elizabeth. It happens to the best of us."

In the house, Sheila paced about the kitchen, her toenails restlessly clicking on the linoleum while drops of blood fell like tears behind her. A dog's tears of longing. Her restlessness made me restless, so we stayed outside. To this day, I remember those sorrowful days with Sheila as *walking the dog*. A seagull looking down on the two of us would have thought, how sad and heavy-laden those two look, the path of their footprints endlessly circling that tattered house.

I could not cry, had not, even when Michael's mother, Bertie, came to my dead mother's side, her sorrow first sounding animalish in her throat, then becoming louder, haunting the house with howling. She seemed to be crying for many losses: some tears for my mother, maybe some for her missing fingers and some, I'm sure, for her youth. A multitude of feelings get tangled in a loved one's death.

My youth thought Bertie's stormy sorrow maudlin, but time would teach me the woman's cry. Some part of me knew this as I watched Bertie shroud my mother in the bed sheet, but at the time, a mantilla of black came down, binding me like a lone fish in a net. I surrendered to loneliness.

Only days before Mother died she said my grandfather *surrendered* to the sea, that the hurricane and rough ocean had nothing to do with his death. *He jumped.*

"Why?" I'd asked, picturing him stepping from the rocking boat.

She said, "For some, there is a loneliness so vast as to make the raging sea welcoming."

"How could that be?"

To help me understand, Mother created a

collection of snapshots: Grandfather in front of the World War II concrete bunker in Cap Gris-Nez, my grandmother barely sixteen, holding up a small, but intricate lace tablecloth that she had made and which my grandfather bought from her in the marketplace; my grandparents as lovers on the sandy beach of Sangatte, sharing French bread and wine on a blanket; my grandmother at my grandfather's departing ship, the White Cliffs of Dover behind her, but not visible because of the dense fog. Mother said Grandmother was pregnant with my father and the lovers had married the night before in a civil ceremony. Grandmother would follow Grandfather back to Stonington later.

"Because of the baby?" I asked.

"No, because she loved him."

"Then why didn't she stay?"

Mother looked off. "Somewhere in the attic, Elizabeth, there is a picture of your grandmother with Marie when she was little. It was after they returned to France. The two of them are beneath the Monument des Bourgeois de Calais. Do you know about the monument, Elizabeth?"

How could I know about a monument in France? I'd never been anywhere. My mind raced over things Mother had shown me in the *Compton's Pictured Encyclopedias* at the library, stopping on the Hanging Gardens of Babylon, The Great Pyramids, Stonehenge,

Colossus of Rhodes. Frustrated, I asked again, "Why didn't she stay?"

Mother looked back, her eyes as clear as glass. "Elizabeth, a woman's life should start new with her husband, but for some it doesn't. Your grandmother was homesick. She was not without guilt, you know. No woman ever is."

No woman ever is.

Those words corralled me, making me picture the wild horses on Sable Island that Mother told me about the morning Father left, even though I hadn't told her he was gone. She said those horses were as free as they could be on that little island, yet some died trying to leave.

"How is that?" I had asked.

"They drown," she said. "Once so many horses were washing up on the mainland that the government sent a team out to investigate."

"What did they discover?"

"That the horses always left at night. It seems strange, doesn't it, Elizabeth? To have such faith in the dark?"

Mother cleared her throat. "They also discovered that if the horses had offspring, they left them behind."

Mother's words drifted around me as if they were colts themselves searching a lonesome shore. "They leave their children behind?"

"Yes, Elizabeth."

"Do male horses leave, too?"

Mother nodded yes, then closed her eyes to hide a tear, but it had already escaped and was streaming down her face, reflecting the pink morning sky outside. Her shoulders curled in, making the shape of a cave around her heart. I knew she was feeling a loneliness so vast as to make the raging sea welcoming. She knew Father was gone.

Part Two

1

I started running with Sheila out Route 15 toward the Deer Isle bridge, keeping track of the days: 129 days since Mother was buried. We took her to the cemetery and laid her with the sailors of foreign waters. Grandfather was next to her on the bare and abandoned knoll, baked by the summer sun that was passing, distancing its warmth as if we, the islanders, were all being abandoned. Huge white rocks were cast about the edge of the cemetery and scattered through the trees; a terminal moraine of unchiseled statues.

Gwen did not come home for Mother's funeral. She had traveled to Florida with a boyfriend and could not afford the ticket home, but Aunt Marie came, hiding her chapped laundress hands with black gloves that matched her black hair that matched the cawing crows scouring the bright skies above. Her lips were painted the red that only French women can wear, no doubt one of her own mother's traits, passed down as surely as the color of one's eyes or hair. Marie's skin was as white as powdery stone. Years later, a photographer's book would reveal to me the statues and statuettes at Père Lachaise. The photographer airbrushed the photographs of the statues' lips violent red. By doing so, he embodied something of the very essence of French women, their capacity to paint, to wrap a silken scarf around their pain, not to hide it, of course, but to honor its beauty. *Here, I paint a heart of painful discovery. Here, I claim it.*

On the bright burial day of my mother, burnt sienna leaves crinkled about us, flickering like painted flames in the trees. Aunt Marie sang the sailor's hymn falsetto. Her lips were so beautiful as to be a world of their own. Red and riverly . . . *Bless those in peril on the sea* . . . Her voice traveled in and out, a plainsong of waves and longing . . . Surely, she must believe all the dead were listening, all the loved ones buried upon that barren hill, and it seemed in that moment she understood the pain of all those gone before her, gathering it to her chest like a twine-tied package. Some say only the holy understand the pain of everyone, but I have seen it weighing momentarily on the faces of certain people, a mixture of empathy and understanding, a loaded down, almost sinking boat of necessary supplies.

Mother used to say, *If you let it, Elizabeth, all the world connects.* Some of her sayings were like tangled lifelines thrown toward me. They were meant to save but took some work.

Looking back to the cemetery, I saw a stray dog panting at Mother's fresh and earthy grave. A ghost of a dog. *Sadie, our Sadie,* we'd all said to Father that day so long ago. "How could you shoot our Sadie?" He said, "Girls, there are many social evils in this world. Read *The Grapes of Wrath.*"

Ninety-seven days since Father made his first and only call: *Mother? Oh, she's dead. Has been and you not knowing. You not caring. Of course, there was no way to reach you. Her face opened in death, Father. It was pretty again. You should have seen it. Oh, no, Father, Gwen isn't here. Of course not, you cured her of this place, Father. Me? I eat macaroni and tomatoes and bread. Me? I'm getting fat on macaroni and tomatoes and Mother's Ganong chocolates. I love their sickly sweetness now, rising in my throat, a twisting curving caramel stream making me forget I'm bleeding inside. Hemorrhaging. No doubt, you've read about people like me. How wonderful to be a character in one of your books, Father. Such scrutiny. But we, you hardly no-ticed. Your girls. As inconsequential as sea anemones: our fingers, our petals like suckers clinging to your back.*

Before Father hung up, he said, "I'll send money, Elizabeth. I'll look after things, don't worry." I suppose he thought those words were like his arms around me, but I was hoping for his return and my rescue. In

85

sweaty restless dreams, we embraced and fell on Mother's grave. I rubbed the muscles on the back of his neck while he cried himself red, the familiar painter's red. I became Mother, bringing him coffee while he worked, resting my head on his chest while he read a tattered paperback, licking his ear, knitting a sweater beside him.

I'll send money. Those words hollowed me out like a bowl. "I simply cannot come home now, Elizabeth. Not now. Someday you'll understand. I'll set things up for you, though."

Running with Sheila, I'd imagine a slaughter, blood spurting from my chest, family blood (all mine that was theirs and all theirs that was mine). I ran in the region above the clouds, my life a wake behind me. Only then could I forget the house of voices, the haunting home, Father and Mother and Gwen. I became unsolicitous there, uttering my own soliloquy of need. Some might call it prayer.

At home, I remained alone except for soft Sheila and Michael MacDonald's nightly visit. His mother sent him to check on me, a sacrifice that she would never fully understand. Sometimes Michael came with a pail of fresh milk, standing inside the door as shyly as the night he'd come to apologize to Mother for firing the puck that shattered her face. I tried to receive him in love as she had, but it was a fraudulent imitation. I felt nothing. One night, I tried to jump-start myself by licking Michael's warm and wiry neck. I lapped at it the same way Sheila lapped at my salty fingers. Warm milk slopped from the pail he held.

After, I unbuttoned my shirt. Michael put the milk pail beside us, then fumbled at my breasts, the first to ever touch me in that way. He smelled of cows, abruptly sour, a smell that reminded me of my hollow sorrow as pungent as vinegar when it rose in my throat. I hated the smell of cows, but wasn't I deserving of it? My travesty of tongue.

I watched Michael's green eyes glaze over as he touched me. Even in their state of lust and luster, they revealed his goodness. The eyes of sanctuary. Fields of green. Eyes that would never hurt me, eyes that would row out for me no matter how thick the fog. Love, Michael told me later, started with those touchings and I know now that is the way certain men can be. So much about touch and feel. Women criticize them, but for some, the way their bodies react is pure love, otherwise they would not react. These are the men to marry.

My body didn't respond. Like the very kitchen I stood in, it seemed trapped in wainscotting. Painted over a hundred times. White yet dull. An imposter of cleanliness.

Later, I would learn of the cream that gathers between a girl's legs. God's dangerous plan. Until then, though, I'd stay as dry as my lacquered eyes and Michael's fingers were like pumice scrubbing me, swelling me; to no avail. For Michael's sake, I faked enjoyment. Julie Ann Sparrow and I had read about the sighing of a woman's pleasure, so I practiced. At the kitchen door. Neither coming nor going, long breathy sighs that slowly cumulated into a thunderous moan, more desperate than the woman's moan of mourning. I clung to Michael, feeling neither clean nor sordid, neither devil nor angel, feeling neither.

Michael whispered, "Are you all right?"

"Of course, I'm all right, don't you know anything about pleasure?"

He blushed and went home, leaving his gray cap on the floor beside the pail. I kicked my twisted panties off, then sat in the bidet of milk. *Wash me down . . .*

After, my clothing might as well have been ashes. *Ashes, ashes, we all fall down.* To cover up was to lie, to hide from my very self. Wandering naked through the cold house, I stood in front of one of Father's paintings, shivering. It hung in the hallway near the stairs. Three-by-five. The day he started it, he sliced his index finger with a shaving blade. Washing the tiny canvas with his

88

blood, the red of his sister's lips, as if some part of him was claiming that color as his heritage, too. *Here, I claim it.* At the time, Mother was in Canada selling her parents' house, a visit that had caused much arguing before she left. Father never wanted her to leave. He thought she might not return. He'd insisted that she leave her skates and we all kept looking at them, hanging on a hook behind the woodstove.

Gwen and I were connecting the old dry dots of paints beneath Father's easel. They looked like wedding confetti. *Why'd you cut yourself, Father? Father, why did you?*

He said, "Every good painting begins with a man's blood."

But we never saw you do that before.

Later, Gwen and I pricked our fingers with one of Mother's sewing needles. How brave we were, watching our blood drip down into the wet white kitchen sink, then swirling it in circles until red flowers bloomed. Poppies. We'd followed Father's lesson of ecology. Edified: *Art, we said. Look Father, we're artists.*

He banged our heads together, then scrubbed the sink clean with his bare hands. The running water washed the very questions from our lips, cascaded us under Father's cold and threatening falls.

Suddenly, I remembered Sadie barking the short sharp barks of warning before Father shot her behind the house, because she didn't return when he called. She was herding a group of children coming from school. He yelled, *Sadie, get up here.* Twice, he called, but I don't think Sadie heard him. The wind was blowing fiercely that day. *A herder, Father. It's her natural instinct to herd the children. Why do you want her to deny it?*

Father turned his back on Mother and Gwen and me to shoot our dog. Sadie's head was tilted and shaped with the question of all our unknown sins. The white line down the center of Sadie's black face looked like an excess of paint dripping. A waste. There was an explosion of red. Not the red of poppies or French lips, but crimson, the true scarlet color of our throbbing hearts, which exploded within us, Father's girls, so powerfully as to create a scent similar to the drippings beneath a butcher's table, both cool and warm, rancid and fresh, still yet flowing.

In that moment, Father rifled us to the rimland of family, gathered us like casualties from a sunken ship. If we had asked why, he would have said he executed Sadie for our sake. Disobedience was not to be tolerated. What if Sadie was out running wild in the fields when you girls needed protection?

What if?

Father propped the rifle over his shoulder and turned to face us. His choir of girls, our mouths opened — o-o-o — but no dirge came out. The silent — o-o-o — germinating seeds within our blasted hearts, growing rounder and emptier from then on. A blithed ovum. *This O, this growing hole, marks the place where a man's love should be.*

Father came into the house, leaned his gun in the corner of his painting room, then turned to Mother's wails and pounding fists. *You bastard.*

He let her beat at him while he steadied her down into the rocking chair before going outside. Mother sobbed into her shaking hands while Gwen gagged and vomited into the sink. The air blossomed with bile. "Why?" Gwen seethed, "why did you marry him?

"Why, why, why?"

"I love him," Mother screamed, her voice echoing through the house, *love him, love him, love him* . . . she stood and walked upstairs. It was the first time I saw her posture limp.

I stood still at the window, thankful Father hadn't shot us, too. Hadn't we all at one time or another disobeyed him? He stood outside smoking and looking at the wild wind and waves and mist coming in over the islands. It was spring, but the air smelled of snow. I pictured myself standing in the wind of my future. Looking away from my own children. Not wanting them to know I was grieving for something beyond, wishing, for something more than the fishing boats and battered houses or the sometimes shabby love of marriage. Wishing to be master of something or someone.

We all ended up in the wind of Father's harsh departing judgments; shattered girls for which he had no use. Even Mother. Memories would be made in the future: Gwen coming to Stonington, glued back together over and over, each aging crack on her face threatening to come undone and show the very glue of her. Married three times, now with another man. A shiny car man named Eldon who teased Gwen for being sentimental when she fell down at Mother's grave like a place she could cover. Gwen maybe more than anyone wore her grief, but not in the way of our French blood. Instead, it was layered like sea dust on the face of a doll, making her look old and worn before her time. Something you think you can wipe away with some care, only to find it has been there too long and left a stain. Gwen, the one who remembered boughs breaking beneath a newborn, a father cursing her natural desires, threatening to kill her first lover if he ever came near our house again, a father shooting her family's beloved dog.

The night of the shooting, Mother took Gwen and me to bed early with her. One daughter on each side, wilted and battered. "There is a God for animals," Mother said, "heaven is a child's sketch of dreams." Then she defiantly and sweetly hummed, *Oh Canada, glorious and free* . . . until Gwen and I fell asleep. In the morning, we asked Mother if we could bury Sadie. She cried when she told us Father had already taken Sadie to the dump.

One winter's night, I could run no more. I'd left Sheila at the house because the night before she'd pulled away and disappeared into the woods. In the distance, the coyotes were howling. She yelped and pulled until I couldn't hang on to her any longer. It was not unusual for local dogs to mate with coyotes. The woods around Stonington were full of coydogs, and a few times the town had even put a bounty on them. Once one had attacked a child playing in her sandbox.

Mr. Sparrow had bred Sheila the day before with one of his studs and in my ignorance I supposed that would end her desire. I was too young to realize that longing can be a meandering and endless stream.

I missed the tug of Sheila's leash. Sometimes it was all that pulled me into the night. Often she forced me to run so fast that I pictured myself flying. That night, the region above the clouds eluded me — no child's sketch of dreams — as did the things behind me: no Stonington, no frozen lily pond with Mother skating, no thumping, scratching blades against the ice, no sweet tobacco smell with turpentine, no cinnamon toast, no sister laughing, no kitchen fire snapping, no knitting needles clicking, no images on my cavernous walls. Icicles grew inside. Rooted themselves like mirrored daggers reflecting all the hurts my parents passed between them, *You. You. You.* My father saying good-bye while betraying Mother at the foot of their bed. *You you you.* . . .

In a recurring dream, Father stood naked facing me. His face had been replaced with Sadie's black-and-white tilted face. Why? he seemed to say. In the dream, I was never sure if I had a gun propped over my shoulder or not. It could have been a flag I was holding. The dream nagged at me.

Years later, I'll tell my husband of this dream and he will say, "Everyone is redeemable Elizabeth, even if we don't believe so at the time." This will be the nature of the man I'll marry. In our ordinary life, these will be the simple and strong things that he'll sometimes say. He'll say, "Elizabeth, there are three things a man can spend all day watching."

"What's that?" I'll ask.

"The sea, fire and his own children."

"Some men," I'll say.

Breathlessly running, I realized I needed to get back to the house of voices, but I had run all the way to the jagged twisting causeway just before the Deer Isle bridge. It was the farthest I'd ever run, almost fourteen miles. My legs buckled and ached beneath me. The stars hung in cold black skies. Sweetly, they could watch me perish. My sweat turned from cool to cold. The winds howled over the causeway. I was shivering, yet sleepy. Still, I turned and started walking back to Stonington.

At the hill where the road narrowed into a dark path between tall spruce trees, I stopped. The wind cracked the pines, the threatening echoing crack of a ship's mast. I thought I heard an owl, but it could easily have been my own voice echoing off the thin ice in the marshlands, *Who?*

The darkness no longer sharpened my senses, it beguiled them, drummed them numb and made my legs as stiff as planks. Mysterious shapes grew around. For the shortest second, I let go in laughter. Laughter that could only be described as fear. Once, Father told Gwen and me that laughing was the most unguarded a person could be. He warned us against it. *Better you remain serious.*

Blessed be your threat of purgatory, child, for it will protect you.

Behind me in the distance, a car hummed. I turned to narrow lights quickly snaking across the causeway. It was a Jeep and when it was closer, I bravely held my thumb out for a ride. Something, Father said, a girl should never do.

But I would run no more. No more.

The driver hesitated, downshifting, slowly stopping ahead of me. Walking into the red beam of brake lights and putting motor, I realized it was a Jeep that had passed me on several of my runs with a driver I did not recognize. According to Father's warnings, I could become a tragedy, I could disappear forever, but it hardly seemed to matter. I imagined the islanders talking: *What was she doing out there that time of night? She wasn't the same since her father run off. And her mother died. No one expected that. Her sister had troubles, too. Got so she'd run with anyone. Her father kicked that one out. Had to. Maybe this one was like her sister . . . Maybe it's bred in the bone . . . Regular coydogs . . .*

The driver leaned over and swung the passenger's door open. I looked in to see a strong square jaw, to smell cedar like the inside of a box, to feel heat hit me like a warm blanket. Piano music played on the radio, rippled my chest open, a silver striker strumming the daggers, making music that could only be described as warm night, the music that beckons something in us all, freedom just beyond the dark water, sweet alluring darkness.

Get in, he said, edelweiss growing at the

edge of his words. I would have obeyed him no matter what. If he had said, Get out, I would have slowly moved back into the bog, into the very things my father taught me to fear. I would have forever stood in the marshlands cloaked in mist. Only a dead tree to those passing. Abandoned. But he said, "Get in." Melodiously.

He'd noticed me before, running. "Your legs are very strong."

"I have my mother's legs," I said as if confessing, as if they were an evil passed on. *Restlessness.*

I breathed deeply: warm woodsy smells, images of a fire crackling, sticky pitch snapping. Glancing sideways, I guessed the driver to be slightly older than my father. In the red gleam from the dashboard, I could see the deep curving downward lines around his lips, lines weighed down by a man's thinking and reminiscing. This would not be a man of *neither* . . . and even then, I felt only, as in Only at times would I crave deliverance.

An Austrian architect who painted with oils for enjoyment. He asked if I would sit for him someday, and of course I did, sneaking off at night from the house of ghosts to the house he was building for a New Yorker out near the great bridge overlooking Eggemoggin Reach.

There, I confess, he laid me in a dank dungeon on lamb's wool . . . stripped down like a baby from a feverish night, my bare back and bottom to him, my arms stretched above me, wrist resting on wrist as if tied. There was a small window behind him where dark streamed in. Whether dream or true, I'd glimpsed a slaughter hook on the ceiling and later when I was older, shuddered seeing a slaughter hook in a Wyeth painting. *You're so white, so beautifully white.*

That first night, though, driving, we only admitted our names to one another. He was Friedrich, but I could call him Frederick, if I liked, most everyone in America did. He told me Elizabeth suited my wild and wavy black hair. "You look Pre-Raphaelite," he said and I smiled unknowingly.

He drove up the hill to my shabby house, splintering gray in the Jeep's lights. It took all my strength to open the door and get out. On our quiet drive home, listening to the piano music and talking the small talk of strangers, I'd felt rescued.

At the great house, the granite wall dripped in front of me as I lay for him in the cellar: dank echoey drips, weepy indecipherable monosyllabic words that made me imagine the valves of one's heart constantly opening and closing. I thought of Mother's bloody tear, pictured it starting in her heart and traveling up along one of those purple veins in her swan throat, circling through the maze of her brain, which was made up of all the skating marks she'd made in her lifetime: overlapping circles, crossovers and tight spins, then that blood pushing down through her broken forehead until she cried that last tear.

A massive cerebral hemorrhage, the death report said.

Frederick's painting strokes were much more definite than my Father's. Tight heavy-pressured strokes, thick with undiluted paint, strokes that would eventually render me back to life. There in the dungeon, I would hear and smell and see again. Not the least, but the last would be to feel a man's love. *Dripping stone, bring him to me. Find, buried in me, a picture no other will paint. Weeping. Change the stick figure, which is the picture I carry of myself. I don't care what it means.*

Be still, Elizabeth.

There, I lay on the lamb's wool, relaxed yet posed, imagining I'd been wrapped in gauze, my senses muffled yet moist, waiting.

Those nights, I returned home reeking of a new world. It was an ancient odor, a closed room full of lilies. Michael often waited at my door. He must have smelled my dank and newfound world, but he said nothing. He lay with me on the kitchen couch stroking my hair while I writhed on his leg, coaxing him to touch me. In the dream house with Frederick, something trickled beneath my stomach, a spring beneath ice.

The distance between Frederick and me created desire. It swelled inside of me and sometimes, I feared, it was so great that he must hear it. The clear yet distant waves one hears with an ear pressed against a seashell. The same desire must have existed between Father and Celise while he painted her. The untouched wanting to be touched, the unpainted wanting to be painted, the unloved wanting to be loved and in my case with Frederick, the virgin wanting to be unvirgined. What girl needed virginity? Is not our youthful awkwardness enough? I wanted to be opened, *unlocked,* but Frederick kept his distance and Michael would only go so far, before pulling away to go home. This was the kindness of Michael's heart and the greed of mine.

In secret. Fourteen nights Frederick painted me. Dungeon nights I could not eat. The remaining death fat above my hips slithered away. Cold, I sometimes shivered until that fourteenth night: Frederick's tongue licked the bottom of my spine so beautifully as to be warmly woken to a dream, twisting over me, up me . . . bathing me in twilight, his lips blossomed on my neck and ear, then back down. Those lips opened my spine like a zipper, kissing my crevice and bottom until he turned my body to face his face, his wrinkled gray eyes watching until I closed mine . . . his lips touching that small pebble between my legs, between my between. Finally, I surrendered as in a drowning death, weak and capsized by the flowing rivulet of cream beneath me, the eddied stream that he would tame, and dam for our pleasure's sake.

He lay me upstairs in his bed in a room with open rafters. Tenderly, he kissed me. "How old are you?"

I could not think. A number did not come. Just the image of a mask with a haunting grin, huge gaping eyes, its lips held in the familiar girlish o-o-o. The missing more compelling than the concrete; the very definition of a blithed ovum.

When I did not answer, he entered me. I tightened. He stopped, studying my face as if he were memorizing something to paint, my slightly crooked nose, my round eyes or maybe the spot at the peak of my upper lip that Mother always called a dewdrop. He began to move, slowly and surely, turning me as slippery and lush as the seaweed shores of my childhood. My inside against him was as smooth and fleshy as an oyster. I closed my eyes . . . *Try not to be afraid* . . .

Oh, Mother, how I miss you.

Remember when we spent the day stepping on the seaweed bubbles, wet and slimy on the rocky shore, they rolled and popped, surrendering sweet sounds beneath our feet, their juice trickling out, already warmed by the sun.

Walking home, we sucked the salty eggs from a spiny urchin. Something Father had taught us. I puckered and twisted my lips. You said, Think of the juice from an orange, a satsuma. Urchins are an acquired taste. Like coffee or wine. You said, And, Elizabeth, it is the acquired tastes that get you in the end.

Why is that? I asked.

Because they have to do with knowledge.

I didn't understand.

You had a line of seaweed tied about your waist to dry; a sash of dulse for later. Your tanned strong legs glistened beneath frayed blue jean shorts. Watching you, I licked the slimy urchin's yolk, saying, Father says we can survive on things from the sea.

You said, Survive is the key word.

The hot wind came up and bosomy waves rolled behind us. Rolling, subsiding, rolling, subsiding . . .

I called out, Do you not like this place at all?

I love it, you said, turning your head slightly. That is what makes it so hard.

I caught up to you, slipping my hand in yours. You said, Only at times do I crave deliverance. Then you stopped to pick up a drying starfish. It was small lying in the palm of your hand. One of its legs was missing. Quick, Elizabeth, run it back to the sea so it can grow another.

I carried it back, rubbing my fingers over its nubby beauty. Its clinging was gone. How wonderful, I thought, to be able to grow back what has been taken

While dressing, I found a spot of blood on the sheet in the bed where we'd lain. Frederick and me. A bloody teardrop. For a moment I smiled, then thought, This is the measly sight that belongs to a girl, a splattering, a warm thimbleful of liquid no more than that within a seaweed bubble, the urchin's yolk. From this a one-way bridge is built. A crossing over without return; a pilgrimage to the land of lush greenery and vines and roots and for as long as she is fertile, she will wait for the sight of her monthly red, for the absence of it creates a fearful picture, a painting not yet on canvas, but predicted, her thoughts as strong as the summer sun on that pried-open oyster.

That night, when I returned home, Sheila and Michael were curled on the mat in front of the woodstove, cinders cindering, the obligatory pail of milk covered with an aging scum beside them, a book of Father's that I'd been reading in Michael's hands. *Jane Eyre.* I didn't wake Michael, but his young face was beautiful. Compared to the face that had just been near, this face would not consume me.

Beauty without the joyful devastation — the sea without challenge, the sea simply for pleasure's sake, a sail out to an island for berries, freshly sweetened by warm days, no room for shadowy rot or subplot or intrigue. No secrets locked in the attic. Even then, looking at Michael, I wanted to atone, but the dungeon had been beguiling yet cold and Frederick's lips were as enticing as exotic fruit. A taste I would not be able to keep from acquiring.

Sheila sniffed the air. A cut above her eye was still fresh-looking and a corner of it was oozing yellow. She'd gotten it the night she pulled away from me and ran into the woods. Patting the top of her head, I wondered if she'd been back to her wild coyote lover or if one time had been enough, if her longing stream had been sated. Finally, she pulled away, looking back at me with girlish, wilted eyes.

On the kitchen table, there was a white envelope with my name and the Stonington National Bank as a return. Four hundred dollars lay inside with a note: *Compliments of your father.*

The small flowery unfamiliar handwriting swilled me in its mouth and spit me out. It was not the tiny precise printing of my father. Still, he'd set a monthly value, punitively delivered to my door like flowers for the injured. Was the amount too little or too much? I left the envelope on the table and went upstairs to Mother's bed where I lay sleepless. More than once, I took the box of babies' clothes from under her bed. Little white leather walking shoes, worn at the toe that both Gwen and I wore, flannel nighties cross-stitched with yellow and pink. So soft and neatly folded with a sprig of lavender, my mother's slender hands almost visible on them, stitching them, sewing them, then gently caressing them upon our soft and innocent bodies.

Naked, I touched my belly still crusty with Frederick's semen, then licked my fingers, tasting what might be ancient sea salt. Is this from where all men come and all men want to return? Escaping the very earth from which they're made.

The buoy bells called through the closed windows, making me imagine cool sea foam touching my face, waves washing over me. *Try not to be afraid . . . think of the moonlit snow prints of a deer . . .*

Night after night, Frederick entered me as if I were a church. There he put me on the altar, his strong hand gently over my mouth, making me face my childish lie of pleasure. *Sssh, Sssh. Wait until you feel something. Only make the sounds you feel.*

"What sounds will I feel?"

You'll know . . . Forty-seven times he traveled over me, his tongue in unison with mine, hyphenated only by his words — *womanchild* — *so beautiful* — *so warm and you've learned to be so wet* . . .

Finally, in the light of a winter's night, one with such bright moonlight that our shadows followed us to his bed, Frederick lifted me up as if to put me on that slaughter hook, lowering me down as if to rescue me, his hands steadying me above his rhythmic love while I swam the irresistible wave of him. Suddenly, I shuddered in a desperate cry that caused my neck and back to arch, my chest to open like a field, my eyes to close. When I opened them, the moonlight was as glossy as icing on the stucco walls.

My mournful dankness melted, a black-winged shadow grew from it and loomed above, flapping until it became the icy scratching sound of my mother's skates, drifting off, leaving behind the mark of that stick-child. When I could hear the skates no more, I caved down over Frederick and stared into the room through the dark prison of my hair. In winter shadows, the ghost of a young girl stared at me, my thrown clothes a bridge between us. My body shook, yet settled into Frederick's. Maybe for some women, love is born from their bodies, too. Frederick pulled me closer, covered us with the sheet and tightened his arms around me.

We went on, night after night. Breathy, breathless. Cool, warm, then hot and sweaty, rolling, subsiding, sliding, withdrawing, spewing, speaking, whispering; *feeling sounds*.

Now, I understood.

In the day, I wallowed in our lily scent, remembered Frederick's strong hands about my hips, blue veins surrounding his wrists like handcuffs. In daydreams, a garden of our replicated bodies grew, flowing foliage and viney flowers that intertwined, then blossomed like lilies near the surface. Without Frederick I might have been tossed to a world of mendicancy, lived forever in a lie to the man above me. Faking sounds. Surely, it took a certain expertise to detect even a girl's sexual dishonesty. All my world became a quiet wish for night. Day was an uphill trek to reach Frederick. I no longer could get up in time for school. The guidance counselor knocked on my door late one afternoon. The house was cold and I made her tea. She talked, but her words came from lips against a closed window; something about my future. Finally, she said she'd make an appointment for me to talk to a senior counselor. One who visited the school monthly.

When I met with him, a bearded man with wiry eyebrows, he wrote the word *distraught* across my file and underlined it. What did the word represent? The death of my mother or the disappearance of my father or was it my nights he alluded to? Such secrets must somehow show.

I felt sensual shame, a lowering of eyes and tilting of head. A dog's pose. When I stood to leave, he said, "You've been through a lot, Elizabeth, take care of yourself."

I knew I would not go back to school. I would spend my time waiting for my lover. I was probably not the first girl to leave school because of this preoccupation. I'm sure Stonington knew many, the tattered island houses soaking these girls up like rain.

Walking home, the image of these girls weighed heavily on me. Maybe that's why the brain floats, I thought, making the sign of the cross, which was something I hadn't done in a long time.

Ich liebe dich, ich liebe dich. Frederick kissed me. These words played at my ears, tickled me in the warmest way. A branding never to be erased. Panting, I lay beneath him, each breath searching for words to whisper back. Only shapes floated in my brain. Colorful flowery sea anemones. As if he knew this, Frederick said, "Say nothing. You are too young."

I learned to come to him swampy and bedraggled. That was the way he wanted me. *Leave your body smells for me. They are so beautiful.*

"What do I smell like?"

A damp orchard.

"What does a damp orchard smell like?"

He was rubbing his semen into my stomach and chest again, staring off, as if beyond he saw a beautiful world that he would never quite reach. He said, "Your broth smells like home."

Home? I wondered then if home is not from where men come, but where they search to go: *A boy is your son until he gets a wife, but a daughter is your daughter for the rest of her life.*

After, Frederick bathed me and washed my hair in a round tub in the corner of his room with the open rafters. When the water became cool, he wrapped me in a thick white towel and lay me on the bed to sleep. When I woke, he was sitting in a chair near the window, sketching me, simple flowing charcoal lines that made the shape of a woman, her face slightly turned to the painter's eye, but not looking at him. He drew me full and alive, a circle of arms and shoulders, wavy hair, clinging fingers. He drew me fuller than I was, he drew me satisfied, dreamy . . .

Sometimes after he bathed me and before he drove me home, Frederick would go down to the dungeon claiming he had an idea that couldn't wait. When he left the bedroom, he took something of the air, so until he returned my breathing remained as shallow as a newborn's. Once I stood in his closet touching his clothes: suede as soft as a baby's face, off-white sweaters woven like a cocoon, corduroy as warm as steam and the handsome smell of leather. The smell that embraces one with promises. Frederick had told me leather was very important to Austrians. I imagined a whole country of leather-clad people, even the children dressed in leather the color of pansies. I looked down at my flannel shirt and jeans. Beneath them lay white cotton panties and a bra with worn elastic. Why would he want me?

And then I asked myself, "Why do you want him?"

The answer lay on my tongue as if, like my taste buds, it had always been there: *His hands. Hands that could restore me, mold me, shape me. Hands I could taste.* At the oddest times, even now, I remember his hands running over my body, bringing me to life, shaping the white curves, aligning my hips, sculpting my breasts with circular firmness, traveling up my neck, then outlining my eyes and nose and lips, and opening my mouth to massage my tongue; his fingers tasting of creamy toffee.

His hands were strong with taut sinewy forearms and when he towered over me, thrusting steadily, veins came out in his hands and arms, and seeped up through his chest and neck and face and sometimes, I saw the veiny maze of night-blue wires that held him together. In those moments, he looked so alone, the veiny maze a barbed wire fence between us.

Frederick and I painted in the dungeon no more, but played in the world I never knew, two seals in an oily iridescent sea. I told Frederick my parents were dead, killed in a car crash, died hanging on to hands and that my brother waited at home for me.

I wove lies of mud and twigs to make a nest. Lies that were as easily portrayed as Father's silly fishing boats. One after another. I suppose this is where my story of danger begins. Me, the empty one. The Liar. I couldn't help myself. I wanted Frederick, but I was no more than a worm wanting to be a butterfly. My portrayals were as flimsy as fishing shacks. Of course, Frederick knew this. Yet he held me firmly with those hands, petting me, turning, rubbing, studying, patiently listening, looking through my childishness. Sometimes grinning, his beautiful square white teeth biting a corner of his lip, watching, his gray eyes glazing. I knew he was seeing stories beyond the ones I told, but I didn't know if they were my stories or his. Sometimes, he tried to teach me, not just about our bodies together, but about other things. Simple things that I assumed most sophisticated people knew:

Leonardo da Vinci invented scissors.

*A New Guinea tribe eat the ashes of
their dead.*
*A Hollywood bed had an upholstered
headboard.*
The word for brown to green is umber.
*In ancient times, they used coffee to
brand animals.*
*French women are notorious for spending
money on skincare and lingerie.*

"I'm French," I said cheerfully.
He grinned.
"Half."

Finally, one night, after serving me fried
porkchops and rye bread, he said smiling,
"Elizabeth, you don't need to tell me sto-
ries."
"If I don't, you won't want me."
He reached over and rubbed my cheek. I
could smell pork grease and pepper on his
fingers. "I'll always want you."
"Why?"
"Your innocence is a drug."
"I'm poor," I said.
"You are a palace."
"I'm empty."
"Yes, but your soil is moist and black."
"Black?" I asked.
"Rich. Anything could grow there. You
have a whole lifetime ahead of you."
He sucked his cigarette slowly, letting the

smoke travel in and out with his easy breathing. It was a look Father often had after one of Celise's visits. That look of disloyalty.

It was the winter of rain. The lily pond never once froze over, leading me to believe my previous life had been a series of dreams and nightmares and now I was in the real world. A world I loved. Often, the air smelled of perpetual spring, making me think that winter would never come again, that Stonington had kissed the lips of a tropical lover, swearing never to return to ice. Sheila's tongue panted in the warm winds. She dug holes around the house and lay in them. Her stomach was dragging with babies. Lying in the wet holes, her white undercoat became so dirty that I made her stay outside. At night, I tied her to the front step while she watched with wild eyes. She paced anxiously as far as the rope would let her and barked when Frederick came to pick me up after dark. Backing away, I'd watch her in the Jeep's lights, digging furiously beside the door. She'd dig for hours, exhausting herself, and eventually there was a huge gaping hole next to the house. A dark and shallow grave big enough for a family.

On those nights with Frederick, the moon arched quickly across the sky. No sooner had he picked me up, then it seemed we were returning, the moon already tucked in behind a blanket of gray dawn. Since telling Frederick I was fifteen, he was nervous about the locals seeing us, so he always picked me up in the dark and dropped me off in the dark, making me imagine myself cloaked and covered.

I teased him about being nervous, telling him that even the beloved lost at sea only warranted a few days searching. *Who cares where I am?*

He said, Statutory rape is not a joke. He said this easily, as familiar as a loved one's name, *Statutory,* but it was as foreign to me as the wood he shipped in from faraway places and used to build the dream house: mahogany from Honduras, cypress planks from Georgia, and Douglas fir from the Pacific Northwest, koa from Hawaii. I told him the islanders didn't care about us; lots of girls were married and having kids at fifteen. "Islanders are different," I said. "You'll see. They have other worries."

His look turned thoughtful. Maybe in another lifetime he understood something of a simpler life and missed it or perhaps he saw my simple destiny. One that couldn't possibly include the streets of New York or the hills of Austria, which he said were as green as the lichen that grew between the rocks of Maine.

During the moonlight, Frederick taught me

to lock my legs around him and be carried away. Rescued. A drowning girl pulled from the sea. His hands made trails about my neck and breasts and bottom. Courses no one had traveled. Courses I hadn't even imagined existed. Watching his hands, I came to think of them as voices. I came to hear them traveling over me, the sweet hush of a voyage in the night.

Until then, I was paper without the glide of ink. I did not understand Gwen's word, *smooth*. There, beneath the open rafters, Frederick wrote a sentence and locked me within his parentheses. No epigraph, no epilogue, just text. A one-word sentence. A world. He nurtured that world with his black and beautiful script, a long loopy *p* and *t* and *g*; *r* for restless; *o* for the shape of a scream; and *eee*'s like waves. *Protégée*. Frederick underlined it, sealed it and for all I know, planned it. I became that word, that world. I embraced it like a foolish girl. A French word, no less. *Protégée . . . Wrap your legs around me.*

Again and again, he bathed me and fed me oranges, which he peeled with a silver pocket knife. I said the word *satsuma*.

He rolled and smoked filterless cigarettes, sometimes offering me a drag, which I sucked in and held, expelling only when my lungs gave me no other choice. I began to

115

picture myself living with him, maybe going back to New York where he said he had an apartment, or even to Austria to meet his mother whom he said could be cold and cruel. He had given me no reason to think he would ever take me anywhere, other than the gift of a green velvet dress, which he brought back from a trip to New York. The dress was too elegant to ever wear in Stonington. Touching its warmth, I dreamed of places he might show me.

The dress laced up the front making my waist look thinner, and it held my breasts bold and soft above the scalloped neckline. Looking at them, one could never call them breasts — they were too beautiful, breathy and alive, almost foamy looking in their translucence.

When I modeled the dress for Frederick one night, his eyes traveled over me so closely that I felt their jewel-like weight. He walked around me, then took a long silver barrette from his pocket and said, "Sweep the front of your hair back." I obeyed and he took me to one of the large windows that faced the Reach. Our reflection was framed perfectly in the long pane of glass. I looked like a girl who might know the interior of castles and turrets, of celebratory dances and rites of passage, but I suppose in the end I was only an ignorant girl. Dreaming.

Frederick looked bold and strong behind

me. He cradled me and kissed my neck, whispering, "I have seen a painting that looks so much like you."

"Where?"

"A Rosetti in London. She is wearing a dress, the very color of this; green water."

"I've never heard of green water."

Frederick kissed behind my ear, then said, "It's rare, but you see it high in the mountains. It's the color of glacial lakes."

"Tell me more about the painting," I said.

"Her name is Proserpine," he whispered.

"Who is she?"

"She is the unwilling wife of a powerful god."

I hoped then that maybe Frederick was asking me to marry him. I let him take the weight of my head and body asking, "What is Proserpine doing in the painting?"

"She's holding a pomegranate, which indicates fertility and the extent of her yearly entombment."

"A pomegranate?"

"It is a round, seedy, sweet fruit. They say it was really a pomegranate that Eve tempted Adam with."

I swallowed. "And entombment? What is that?"

"Ah," he said, which was a word he usually used when I explained something to him, "to be locked away."

Frederick went on to describe the pomegranate in Proserpine's hand. "There's a bite taken out of it, revealing its center, which is the color of a blood orange."

He lifted the back of my dress, folds of velvet that clung to me like humid weather, then he pressed his warm palm between my legs and rubbed flatly, steadily, whispering, "A blood orange is the color of your center."

He ravished my neck with his lips, circling his tongue inside my ear, all the while still rubbing. I let my head roll to the side, watching our reflection until I was dizzy and closed my eyes. He laid me on the cool blue stone floor and lifted the front of my dress up, finding me buried beneath it and saying, "The pomegranate has a stem shaped like a crown."

My thoughts of Frederick became a staple then, replacing the macaroni, the canned tomatoes, and the bread. Replacing my father, my mother, my sister. His physical love was a circular staircase I climbed to see a new world, my Colossus of Rhodes. Of course, one cannot live up high forever. One must come down and it happened when Frederick said a woman was coming to visit him for the weekend.

A woman?

Bluntly.

Did I not know this would happen? He was older. There was a life before me. He would see me when she left.

We were naked on his bed.

"What will I do?" I asked.

"What do you mean?"

"What will I do without you?"

His face was crinkled like old paper. I saw my vulnerabilities written on it. Etchings in a cave. *Rescue me.*

He dressed silently and walked away, a basket of black birds appearing at his side. A nest of my surrenderings. "What about the paintings of me?" I called out.

"I've hidden them," he said, without looking back.

I knew then that the moonlit snow prints of a deer were simply evidence of an animal running. Picturing another man leaving, I cried, "Please don't go."

I believe he pretended not to hear.

My word came to me, my meaning, like the backward fall from a chair — Protégée: *one who is protected or trained and whose life is furthered by a person of experience, prominence, or influence.*

She, the woman, stayed for two and a half weeks and only once in that time did I see Frederick. Falling, I began walking the dog again. Sheila's legs had grown weak from being tied to the house and she'd been chewing at one paw. It was raw and crusted with blood. She was expecting her first litter, but she limped along looking as worn as the battered mother-bitch of dozens.

One still and foggy morning, Frederick drove up beside us. I was at the turn in Route 15 where you first catch sight of the bridge. The place I'd reached the night he picked me up hitchhiking. I kept walking, thinking maybe Frederick had come as a dream. A haunting. Gwen did. Mother did. Father did. Why not Frederick? Besides, to stop walking would have been to collapse, to fall at his feet and beg, so I continued even though my upper legs were as wobbly as my loyal dog's. Sheila's ears perked and she began to growl. I jerked her leash, scolding her, but her eyes remained wild while she whiffed at the air.

"I love you," Frederick called over the Jeep's putting sound.

It was the first time he said these words to me in English. The sound of them, deep and definite, made me desperate for him; words as sure as shapes in a rock. His eyes were pleading. He looked so tired and old that for the first time, I saw him as someone who had traveled through his life at a very fast pace. With all his knowing, his sleight of hand, there was a look of regret, of things done or left undone. I wasn't sure which.

I stopped. "Why did you let her come here?"

The fog was suddenly denser, the air more humid, wandering between us, putrid with the scent of sea roses. Frederick stared at the road ahead, then back to me. "She's my wife," he admitted.

Those words turned the fog cold. In it, I was beclouded, bedimmed, befogged. I was eclipsed. I was entombed.

He looked at me apologetically before shifting gears hard and driving off. The Jeep swerved across the causeway, shifting and racing to the bridge where it would climb then disappear, its distant motor quickly fading to the other side.

His wife. Eventually, I'd learn that she was much more than his wife. A wife can be replaced. My father had proven that, but how do you replace those familiar with your irresistible sins? Surely not with a new and inchoate concubine.

Back home, I got out the puzzle of the European castle, but could not fit the pieces together. I needed my mother's help. In many ways, all the new pieces of my life, pieces that revealed themselves when a girl crosses over that bridge of discovery, couldn't fit together. I tried to recall Mother's lilty voice, her lips coasting over Elizabeth Bishop's poetry while we sat watching the summer schooners, but I couldn't bring her voice to mind. Now, she moved in a silent film.

Later I searched the house until I found the book of poems, making myself read from worn pages, "The Fish" — someone catches an old and tattered fish — one with many hook scars on its lips.

What would Mother tell me about Frederick? To get away from him. That a man with that many scars on his lips would never be landed by someone like me. The only time I'd missed Mother more would be later when I bore my children, crying the true woman's cry. Do we ever stop wanting our mother? The first time Frederick made love to me, I dreamed of going home to Mother. I wanted her to be there, I wanted her to tell me I was still a clean and lovely girl. When I was older, I shared this with Julie Ann Sparrow and she said, *Elizabeth, that's normal. The first night I had sex with a boy, I went home after and slept like a baby right next to my mother. Of course, I had no idea I was pregnant.* She blinked her eyes as if to hold back tears and said, *Beginner's luck, I guess.*

It reminded me of Gwen. After Father sent her away, Mother took me to Helena's Ledge west of the village on the road to Burnt Cove. We walked to the top of the first hill on Main, then turned on Greenlaw Road, and entered a narrow path where a NO TRESPASSING sign was posted. Mother rushed ahead until we reached a mountain of large bleached stones, smoothly piled on top of one another. We climbed up a steep trail, hanging on to tattered trees that insisted on growing through the cracks of the rocks. The ledge was high, a place where an eagle might build its nest. To the right, the sea was wide open before us, an expanse of navy waves and whitecaps and the odd fishing boat that appeared to be very small. To the left was the village. Apparently, Helena had thrown herself from the ledge many years ago after watching her lover's ship depart. Mother said you could look down and see the shape of Helena on a smaller ledge below. She hung on to me while I inched forward to look down. It was a long, straight drop. If you jumped and survived, there would be no way to climb up the smooth granite. "I don't see anything."

"It has to be low tide," Mother said, pulling me back.

"What else do you know about Helena?" I asked.

We sat down together. "They say she was pregnant."

"Did they ever find her?"

"No. I suppose she floated out with the tide."

"Why are you telling me this, Mother?"

"To warn you."

"Against babies?" I asked.

"Oh no." She smiled. "Against certain types of love."

"What type?"

Mother looked down, kicked a few pebbles from the ledge. They rolled to the edge and disappeared. "The kind that devastates us, Elizabeth."

"Is that the kind of love you have for Father?"

Mother looked out to the sea.

"Is it, Mother?"

She chewed her bottom lip, nodding yes just once.

In time, Frederick's wife went home to New York and he wooed me back. It didn't take much. My throat filled without him. Silty. I bruised with the slightest touch. I could not bathe with no love to bathe away and besides, what if he came to get me? I did not want to smell clean. I wanted to be soiled, more soiled than a girl should ever wish to be for any man. When he touched me that first time after his wife left, I opened like a heated rose.

A carelessness eroded; on both our parts. It could have easily been called despair. *Distraught.* Frederick took advantage of my fear of losing him. Sometimes his foreign words slashed about my face while we made love and once he scratched my back so hard that he left bloody and jagged marks. After, he kissed them and bathed me, soothing the scratches with a warm washcloth. Frederick didn't surrender easily anymore. He thrashed with desperation, pushed my hair back from my eyes, wanted the lights on, ignored the rhythm he'd so patiently taught me, *his good girl.*

I tried to assimilate, but it was a reunion with a stranger. My reflection was no longer in his eyes, they were murky now, held back and under. Something had left a residue, making him as slippery and sullen as the fish that was used to slipping away.

I missed him most when we were together, naked with the warm film of our bodies. Often, just before we made love, there was some sort of promise, nothing spoken, but the lingering of a time gone by, the feeling of anticipation one gets opening a photo album.

One moon-filled night, Frederick walked me through the house that was almost finished. From beginning to end, as if it were a story he needed to tell me. We entered through the heavy doors that faced the huge window that looked out onto the sea, and from there we spiraled down into sunken rooms and around corners. So many of the rooms had been darkness until then, but now clear intense track lighting poured down the white stucco walls, highlighting a collection of daggers and swords and a golden pair of scissors.

The kitchen had ornate salt and pepper shakers and there was a gorgeous line of heavy-stemmed wineglasses above the sink. Telephones had been put in and they rang at odd times of the night as if to awaken the house, as if to never let it sleep.

There was a dark hook for a painting above the huge Sherwood Pink fireplace. Frederick said the owner was coming that weekend and would bring a painting with him. At the owner's request, the house would have only one piece of art. I thought of the Rosetti Frederick had described and wished it could hang there, wished I could see it, but maybe wished more that a like image of me could stay in that house forever.

A round red library off the living room had been filled with books and music, and a single low leather chair sat in the center. "Will only one person live here?" I asked.

"No, the owner will bring his mistress and their son."

His mistress and their son? Then why is there only one chair? Why is there no place for them?

Bravely, I asked, "Is a mistress always invisible?"

Frederick looked at me, slightly flushed. He took my waist and gently backed me against the rough stucco wall. His hands searched frantically through my clothes as if he had misplaced something valuable beneath them. Before, he'd peeled my clothes off as expertly as he peeled oranges, but not now. There, with the bright white lights and Frederick smelling of cigarettes and sultry sweat, I was never more an islander. This is the way I imagined drunken men groped at their wives making the faces of their offspring misplaced and eschewed, mimicking the very slap on their mother's wombs. Is that what my mother meant by love that devastates?

At times, I couldn't help but search the great house. Like Frederick now, it seemed aloof and full of secrets. When we weren't lying naked together, Frederick became more poised and distant, as if he had applied all the rules of architecture to himself. Now his proper lines were something to be studied and admired, but never figured out.

I became wild, gnawing at my fingernails, which Frederick said was ruining the looks of my hands. I felt desperate, the same way I felt when Father rendered me helpless. I tried to memorize Frederick's face, the cedary smell of his neck, his warm reedy stiffness inside me, his coaxing hands, the recent fever of foreign words.

When he took a shower or was busy with a phone call, I sneaked about the house. At the back of his closet, behind his beautiful clothes, I found a strange belt, worn and thick with steel attachments. It seemed like it might be used to contain a wild animal. I knew then something was hidden away, a secret tucked like madness in an upper room.

Many years later, I would read that the mystery to life is that no living creature is predictable. *Anything has wild in it and any-thing can go wild again.* I would think back to my time with Frederick and how he changed so quickly.

The writer went on to describe something called an ankus, a tool used as a prod, which has a history in domesticating great animals. She also described a gold ceremonial ankus used by King Ianmeiaya to break the virgin women in his Burmese court, and a stained ankus cut from the tree Christ bore on the Via Dolorosa, with inlaid mother-of-pearl. I wondered if Frederick's ankus was something planned for me or perhaps, like his sullen mood, it, too, was remaindered from his wife's visit.

Once when he was unable to make love, he drank a bottle of Riesling, then slept open-mouthed at the foot of the bed. I listened to his breathing, while holding the empty bottle and memorizing its label: *Neumayer Traisentaler Riesling.* It smelled like violets and made me picture the lichen-colored hills of his home. He had said even if you didn't see the cows in Austria, you always heard their bells ringing.

"Are they like buoy bells?" I'd asked.

"No, their sound is somehow deeper and thinner. Most things are different there."

When I was sure he wasn't going to wake from his violet breath, I went down to the dungeon. The heavy door whined open and a blast of chilling air rustled over my bare legs. New paintings lay cast about, every one of them a mask of vibrant color. Some so real that human eyes seemed to stare out from behind them and some a cryptic rendition of half-person, half-dog.

The curious mask paintings frightened me, but they didn't stop me from wanting Frederick. As much as I'd wished they would. They were something I wanted to see behind. They ignited more desire for him, which made me feel guilty. *Guilt*. The thing that Mother said every woman had.

Our lovemaking became a confused struggle, a melee in which I was battling many things. His roughness sometimes created a moat around my heart, a reserve, a reservoir reserved. If he managed to be satisfied, the veiny prison on the surface of his body took hours to disappear. After, I tried to lie in his arms as I had before, but he often turned away saying I was acting like a needy child.

Only one more time did he hold me as if I meant something to him. We were in his bed and he was gently smoothing down my hair. "I love your wild hair," he said, then confessed he'd made a terrible mistake with his wife.

"By cheating with me?" I asked.

"Yes," he admitted, "but also I've done things with my wife that men usually go outside of their marriages to do."

"What kind of things?"

He stroked my cheek. "We have certain rituals," he said.

I thought of the ankus, but said nothing. He said, "I've treated her like a mistress."

"And me?" I asked bravely.

"You," he said, "you have been my wife." *You have been.*

"In what way have you treated me like your wife, Frederick?"

He pulled me on top of him, massaging my bottom and back with both his hands, then his fingernails traveled softly up and down my spine. "I've tried to protect you from who I really am."

When I returned home that damp morning, I heard Sheila lapping and chewing in the dark hole she had dug. I reached inside and turned the yard light on. Sheila was lying in the shallow grave with three bloody and slimy pups. Beneath their afterbirth, they were the color of her. Black faces with white and black bodies. Her muzzle was shiny and bloody from washing them. She looked up, then rested her nose on a fourth, limp pup beneath her chin. It was smaller than the rest and golden in color, the obvious runt, sired at a different time by a different father, probably by the coyote she'd escaped into the woods to see. She nudged the pup with her nose, rolling it over so I could see its black eyes partially open and dry. There was a slither of mucus about its lips.

I ran to call Michael. After several rings, Bertie answered, and when I said Sheila had had her pups, could she send Michael right away, she said, "Yes, de-ah, I will, but don't you touch those pups. If you touch them too soon, the mother won't care for them."

When I went outside, Sheila had left the three healthy pups in the hole and disappeared with the dead one. Every shadow and nuance of light had become Sheila moving away as if all about the yard black dogs were slipping away, dogs holding the souls of the dead.

When Michael appeared in the shadows, I ran toward him crying, "One's dead."

"It's okay," he said, wrapping his arms around me. "I'll take care of it."

"No, you can't touch it," I cried hysterically, wailing and pulling away, crying more than anyone should for a dead puppy. Grief like a key or a mitten can easily be misplaced, revealing itself later when you least expect it. Is that what Frederick was doing earlier while confessing his mistake with his wife? Mourning?

The day Gwen fell on Mother's grave crying, the shiny car man said, "Let bygones be bygones, sister." He called her "sister." I hated that. She was nobody's sister but mine;

one of the few things I could claim.

Later, Gwen said, "Mourning is wishing, Elizabeth, wishing so many things were different."

The sun was breaking orange over the water when Sheila appeared in the yard, nose to the ground, without her dead pup. Maybe she'd eaten it, wanting to keep it close to her forever.

Sheila lay down in the hole and let the other pups whine and nurse. She licked them while they suckled. "It's better the coydog died," Michael said. "They can't be trusted."

We were watching Sheila and her pups through the screen door. Michael slipped his arms around my waist and when I turned to him, there was a dark shadow of whiskers about his face and his eyes reflected the rising sun's fire. He said firmly, "I would have had to drown it."

Suddenly, I saw all the things Michael was capable of doing, quietly. Duty and loyalty were bred in him. He kissed me. I kissed him back, then we kissed as if looking for some part of ourselves in the other. Our front teeth knocked and our tongues were restless and fast, too fast for real pleasure. His innocent way seemed to be the very thing I needed. There would be no past tense with him. We kissed until the lobster boats were revving in the harbor and spitting water from their bilges.

That night and for twelve nights following, I waited for Frederick to retrieve me. Michael came and sat quietly in the kitchen. He seemed to have lost something, too, or maybe he was just respectful of my mourning.

During that time, I tried to call Frederick but the line was always busy. I imagined that his wife had come back or maybe he'd found another island girl.

Morning, noon and night, the three remaining pups whined at their mother's side. Maybe that was the nature of pups or maybe Sheila didn't have enough milk for them. Maybe she was mourning for the dead one, making her milk as dry as white dust. I wanted to crawl in beside Sheila, hide in a pup's skin and be part of her family, even if it was a sad one. There had to be some comfort in mourning together.

On the thirteenth night, Frederick pulled into the yard. It was midnight and I was just getting out of a bath of grimy water. I dressed quickly and ran outside. Later, Gwen would tell me this was a big mistake, that I should have told him to get lost, but I couldn't. I jumped into his Jeep as if we'd never missed a night together.

"The owner has been here," was all he said.

There was no warning of what he had in store for me, but later I would know that in our absence from one another, he'd spent as much time thinking of me as I had thinking of him. The Jeep was stuffy so I rolled the window down. The spring peepers were singing in the misty fields and the smell was moist and nightly. I immediately regretted the breeze, though, because it blew my clean soapy smell through the Jeep.

When we pulled up to the great house, I was amazed to see it so beautifully lit. Light fixtures in the shape of black eagles hung downward and white light beamed from beneath them, lighting the stucco house with streaks of white that also lit the freshly planted mugho pines that circled the house like chubby children. The house was circular and I marveled at Frederick's ability to build something without edges, setting it amid the tall domestic pines, making it look like a smooth white stone that had always been on the shore of Eggemoggin Reach.

"The owner must love this house," I breathed.

Frederick only nodded.

He led me inside, then downstairs toward the kitchen. We usually went directly to his room, one of the three bedrooms off the main entrance upstairs.

"What's wrong?" I asked.

"You tell me."

"Tell you what?" I stopped on the bottom

step. He was in a huge open space and behind him, the moon was rising over the Reach, making a wide path ripple on the water. "What have I done?" I asked.

"You bathed," he said accusingly.

For the first time since Father shot Sadie, I was afraid of a man. Frederick's accusatory tone was like an X ray clicking, revealing flaws that even I didn't know existed. Painters like my father and Frederick knew the framework of people, the skeleton, putting them at an advantage when confronting someone. My mind raced. I tried to keep calm, saying, "I thought you found someone else. That's why I took a bath. I didn't think you'd come back."

He smirked, shaking his head and walked on, saying with a tired and gravelly voice, "Let me show you something."

I followed him to the small sunken living room where a fire of driftwood was barely burning beneath the shiny cave of pink granite. A sectional sofa covered in bleached sailcloth surrounded the fireplace.

Frederick turned. "Look up."

Above the fireplace hung the painting Father had done of my mother. The one with her damaged face, the joyful skating scene imprinted on her gray and deathly forehead like a punishment.

Seeing it again captured me in that stormy day Mother sat for Father, fish simmering on the back of the woodstove, winds howling. Father studying Mother's face the way Frederick was now studying mine. "Your father isn't dead," Frederick said flatly.

"No, but my mother is."

"And you don't have a brother," he said, his voice as hollow as a freshly dug grave. "It's someone else with you at night."

Frederick moved toward me, wrapped his arms around me. He burrowed his face into my hair and breathed deeply. "The owner thought it would be a good idea to have some of the local officials come by and see the house."

"Why?" I asked.

"Well, let's just say, we're not really up to code, here. For one thing, Elizabeth, I built the house too close to the water."

"Why?"

He placed his hands on my back and squeezed me so tightly that I felt the outline of his ribs and belt buckle, then he said almost apologetically, "The house would be too common set back from the shore."

I breathed his woodsy skin, looking to the rippling moonlit water that almost touched the bow of the house. "You weren't supposed to build it this close?"

"That's right, Elizabeth, but it's better to ask forgiveness than permission."

He licked my neck, then bit my earlobe hard. I tried to pull away, but his arms were solid around me. He said, "Tell me about the boy at your house. Does he touch you?"

I could hear the sly smile in Frederick's words, the slightly curved lip of something planned.

"You don't have a brother, do you, Elizabeth? One of the men visiting told us all about the artist's family and their many tragedies. You lied to me."

"He's just a neighbor," I said. "Our mothers were friends."

"Ah," he breathed, his breath bitter with the wine of nights before. He let go slightly, rocking me back and forth. "How should I punish you?"

I wondered if I should pull away, but before I could gather a plan, Frederick's hand traveled under my shirt and pinched my nipple hard.

"Should I rape you?" he whispered.

I swallowed, then said weakly, "Why? You have me."

He lightened up on my nipple, twirling it like a thought between his fingers. "Because you're a whore, Elizabeth."

"I love you," I said so faintly that even I didn't believe it.

"Ah."

And in that "ah," that two-letter "ah," I heard the sarcastic inflection of a man's honor, the short straight muzzle, the raising of a gun to a dog's head, a thick line of anger drawn and used as a path to escape.

He took me to his bed and he was rougher than he'd ever been, but I didn't resist, so it couldn't be called rape. I accepted it as punishment for lying. While he twisted and turned me, I listened to the March wind, a single coyote's howl riding on it.

After, I slept tired and sore, wrestling with the night that lay as heavy over me as Frederick's recent thrashing, thinking, *I shouldn't come here anymore.*

In the morning, I woke with my hands crossed over my bare stomach. My hair flowed in two dark streams over my breasts. I listened for Frederick, but the house was so still that I knew it was empty. I dozed in and out of sleep, hoping each waking would find sounds of him on his way to me, words of apology sweet on his lips.

It must have been noon when I raised myself up and my long hair fell onto my lap, no longer part of me. For a moment, I thought I must still be sleeping, dreaming, but when I touched my head, more hair fell away. I slid across the bed, stumbling to the bathroom, leaving my black hair in a scattered path behind me.

In the mirror, a pale peaked face with a sheared head stared back, a prison face, the ghost of a girl. I tilted my head, the questioning tilt of Sadie before she was shot. Frederick had cut my hair so closely to my head that in places, my milky scalp showed through. The sight of it reduced me to the image I carried of myself, the stick drawing, rendering me alone and entombed.

When I found the strength to look away from the mirror, I went to Frederick's closet, somehow knowing before I opened the heavily carved door that the hangers would hang as bare as skeletons. Standing there, I cried. Foolishly mourning Frederick more than Mother's dying or Father's leaving or Gwen's banishment. This is the conceit of youth.

After Frederick left, no blood came down. Foolishly, I'd trusted him. This is the misfortune of youth.

Of course, it was Michael who would marry me on a November night, eight months pregnant. This is not your baby, I said. *No one will know that but us.* Filthy, I'd been holding out for Frederick's return, even though it had been months since I walked home from the great house, sheared as a sheep, shivering, knowing that cruelty did not guarantee the return of hatred just as love did not guarantee the return of love. Night after night, I dreamed of Frederick coming back to rescue me. His footsteps were on the stairs, his shape in the shadows at the foot of my bed. He'd become another ghost, his voice always traveling just beneath the winds outside. When I slept, his fingers painted bloated words of love and commitment on my body: a graffito that stained like wine and held me drunk beneath a rosy surface. Of course, I was filling with amniotic fluid, steadily, the way a rain barrel fills with water over the summer. I thought the fullness was simply loneliness. My breasts swelled above my heart and were tender to touch. My nipples turned the color of bruises. If I caressed them, they sometimes cried yellowish flowery tears.

I never imagined my body changing beneath me as if it were another world, expanding then erupting; the earth of me quaking, my mind dividing between joy and pain, alone and not alone, girl and woman, mother and child, and the jarring realization that from a girl's point of blood onward, the opportunity or misfortune to divide is always there, lurking like a stranger.

Part Three

1

In September, Bertie found me listless and dehydrated in my bed. My protruding stomach beneath the white sheet must have been a shock to her, but she never let on. She woke me by rubbing my cheek, her fingers smelling of kneaded dough, then washed me, fed me broth through a straw, and had Michael carry me to their house. When Michael lifted me from the bed, I looked back at the sheets the way the souls of the dead look down at their bodies, and there the dirty shape of me lay; a circular outline as clear as a fossil on a rock.

Bertie put me in Michael's bedroom above the kitchen and nursed me with the attentiveness of a good mother. She'd nurse me many times after that, teaching me to accept the onset of labor, to breathe through transition, to push with all my strength a child into this world. With my second child, she'd say, *Once you learn the rhythm of birthing, Elizabeth, it will be like making love*. This was shocking. First, it was impossible to associate such pain with pleasure and secondly, I couldn't picture Bertie as a lover. She was a mother, a wife, a worker, but it was hard to imagine her beneath Mr. MacDonald, the tall thin man who moved about his family so quietly. Most of the sounds that came from him were secondary; work sounds: chopping wood on the old tree stump beside their house, stoking the fire in the woodstove, wiring a lobster trap together; his scrawny hands chapped and cracking and slightly pink like the talons of a swooping eagle.

Watching Bertie's hands should have taught me she was a lover. Even with two fingers missing, her hands were pliable and willowy while the rest of her was as full and round as the bread dough she kneaded. Her hands received my newborns before anyone else and she had carried their afterbirth and wrapped it in a towel as if it were sacred, sometimes saying, *This is the heart of heaven.* Then, those lithe hands gently washed me down and slipped each swaddled baby beside me to nurse. *Elizabeth, nothing satisfies like a new baby nursing at your breasts.* She whispered this, understanding full well that even newborns are sensitive to the music of their caretakers. *You must hush them into the world.*

Bertie was right — sweet perky lips gently coaxing your milk can satisfy even a selfish woman. She watched me with each of my babies, her hands pressed together beneath her chin. In those moments, her longing expression said *she* was more than capable of surrendering to a child and what she tried to

144

teach me over time was if one is capable of that, one is capable of surrendering to a man. In her way Bertie was saying, *You must learn this, Elizabeth. It's the way of a woman's life. Otherwise, you will have nowhere to go when your children are grown or, Lord forbid, gone. You must be able to return to your husband openly.*

Bertie MacDonald was so plain, yet a gardenlike generosity blossomed from her, a willingness to accommodate others without her ever appearing crowded or shaded from the necessary light. Bertie was not only the hardy long-awaited hostas, ferns and moss, but at times she was as delicate and beautiful as the precious and elusive lilies at the lily pond. Her white skin was softly crinkled silk and about its edges glowed a flowing pink, be it from work or heat or joy or sadness.

Always, Bertie rose early to make pancakes or biscuits and morning tea for Mr. Mac-Donald and Michael. Even with my presence in her home and the eventual presence of my children, Michael somehow remained hers — floating quietly and gently like a buoy near her. Once, a tourist asked what kept the buoys in the harbor from floating away and I replied without hesitation or resentment, "Carefully tied ropes."

If the weather was particularly cold, Bertie would bake a pot of beans during the night, so the men would have something hearty to take to sea. She'd doze while sitting in the rocking chair beside the woodstove, so as not to let the beans burn, checking and adding water during the night. Nestled in our small bedroom above the kitchen, Michael would sometimes say how wonderful the warm beans would taste later. I'd picture him and his father out there floating on rolling waves with no horizon to watch, eating the molassesey beans from home. I've often wondered what men think of when they're at sea. If they have the same worries as their women do about them not coming back, or if they suddenly feel free of all that binds them to the land. Years before, Father had told Mother that Ahab was a divided man, at odds with his own mortality, at odds with the grief in the world, at odds with his own incapacity to enjoy the world's fair show, and therefore be content. Earlier, they'd had a fight and Father's explanation of Ahab seemed to be his way of asking forgiveness as if within the story of Ahab, all men were explained. Mother said, "For crying out loud, Peter, how many women have read *Moby Dick*?"

At first, I didn't know if Michael had a place of contentment, but I wished it for him. Sometimes in the early morning, we lay in bed listening to the howling winds rattle the windows. We never talked about him not returning from the sea, but I believe it was always on our minds and at times this threat intensified our contentment with one another. Perhaps the same way it intensified Bertie's and Mr. MacDonald's. Surely, like us, they sometimes made love under the threatening cloud of loss. A woman probably surrenders her body then, because if anything should happen to her man, she wants to be the last one he remembers. Maybe that is why so many babies are born nine months after men go to war. That kind of surrendering has to increase the chances of a baby. How could it not? The sweetest part of a woman is revealed and laid out before him — an enticing and beckoning path in which she creates a desire in him to return.

In our years together, Michael's slender body broadened as did my hips, having borne four children. Michael became an ample lover. Like his physical broadness and strength, his love for me was bountiful and we started many dark mornings with his hands under my flannel nightie, so many that the breaking sun became synonymous with our lovemaking, unlike the memory of Frederick, which was synonymous with the dark. Michael's face skin was warm from its many days in the fisherman's sun and when his children were born, one girl and two boys, they had the same warmth, as if even the places we travel are passed onto our children. I often thought of that when I was holding one of them and Michael was late coming back from fishing. I thought I was holding the place where he was at that very second and by holding our child closely, I would steer him safely back to us. Once, while waiting for Michael, I napped in the kitchen rocking chair, resting my hands against my tight stomach, which cradled *our* first unborn baby. Dozing, I dreamed of an elegant red horse with amber eyes racing toward me. The horse had its mouth bound, making its eyes look bright and fierce. The closer the horse got, the harder its hooves beat against the ground. When I woke, panting from the dream, Bertie said, "My de-ah, are you all right?"

"Oh, Bertie, I dreamt of a red horse."

My first baby, the one which belonged to Frederick, was six months old then, and she was sleeping in her swing with her cheek against a soft pink doll. Bertie looked at her saying firmly, "It is a white horse that means death, Elizabeth, not a red one. A red horse is war."

It so happened that Michael and Mr. Mac-Donald did have trouble that day. Apparently, Michael was driving the boat and Mr. Mac-Donald was letting out a lobster trap on a new pulley system when his gloved hand became caught. Michael watched the line pull at Mr. MacDonald's hand, then twist and pull the rubber glove into the sea. Later, Michael told me that he thought the line had severed Mr. MacDonald's hand and for a split second, his heart literally stopped.

Shortly after the line incident, a patch of Michael's dark hair turned white. The patch was just over his right ear and shaped like a swimming child. Sometimes this happens to people who drown and are then revived: Their hair turns white as if in those drowning moments they were thrust forward into an older life. In Michael's mind, he must have traveled under the water with Mr. MacDonald's ghostly hand. I imagined him diving in and searching frantically for the missing hand, frantically mistaking sunbeams and shadows for its severed presence.

After the incident, wrinkles also came about Michael's eyes, but they were still the loving eyes that rescued me from my stained and dirty bed. Over the years, his loyalty embroidered itself in me, simple shapes of dogs and children and fishing boats, stitches that made me strong and family worthy. When he first carried me to his bed, I was nothing but threaded gossamer thrust upon an unfamiliar shore. And it took so long for me to mend. Surely, every day he felt my shreddedness.

Our wedding was a sad and desperate celebration, children playing at being grown up. Me, looking like a pitiful doll with my chopped-off hair. It had grown a bit and knotted in tight curls that resembled a mass of black caterpillars, impossible to comb. On my wedding day I refused to look in the mirror. I stepped into the velvet green dress Frederick had given to me, tied it tightly over my pregnant belly and walked with Bertie to the Methodist church. The early evening sky was a dense veil of gray and behind it a half-moon shone above the harbor, as if through frosted glass.

While the minister united us, I stared into the white carnation on Michael's dark lapel. I knew his mother had pinned it there, because the straight pin was so perfectly hidden, the not so pretty thing tucked beneath the beautiful surface. It was the way she often hid her missing fingers, her pretty and perfect hand resting so gracefully on the wounded one.

After the wedding ceremony, the townspeople gathered at the Legion Hall where a potluck supper was followed by two local fiddlers playing. Aunt Marie was there with her new husband, Patrick (a wealthy patron she had met in the hotel where she was a laundress), and Gwen made the trip with them having returned alone from Florida, looking forlorn in her flimsy black skirt and pasted-on pink fingernails. She was twenty, her face tanned the color of cinnamon, her eyes heavily circled with deep blue eyeliner, the layered dark blue of a drowning sea. Obviously, Aunt Marie hadn't been able to influence Gwen with her French style, or perhaps Gwen simply knew it would be wasted on the many different yet similar lives she would choose to live on the shores of Maine. Always a broken-down car or propped-up fishing boat in her yard, always promises of a future that was somehow expected to appear like a visit from God, and frankly with the men Gwen chose it would have taken a miracle to change the courses of their lives. They were made of sleeping days, government checks, early fried suppers and long endless evenings of drinking beer. Some were better looking than others and some treated Gwen better than others, but each seemed to have long ago given into a life of disappointments. Eventually, they would push Gwen from their lives, adding her to their list of disappointments. None of them was at all interested in finding the girl tucked beneath the painted eyes.

Our wedding guests made Gwen dance with a box on her foot, a custom of the islanders when a younger sister marries before an older one. She was drunk, but clumsily made the best of it, her limp brown hair flying about her face. They clapped and laughed while I held back tears, for her life, like mine, seemed that it would always be a tattered grace, impossible to restore or hide. Earlier, she had expressed disappointment at not being married. She said, "None of them keep their promises." Still, in Gwen's dance, there was something of Mother, something whimsical like the momentary sighting of wings. Perhaps these wings only appear on the backs of dreamers. Perhaps they are not wings but the shredded gossamer of one's dreams — a floating collage that at certain times tries its best to lift you from the ground.

Aunt Marie must have noticed me watching Gwen, because she rushed to my side, telling me how beautiful I looked in my velvet dress. She said, "You look like a painting of a Tyrolean princess."

"Tyrolean?" I asked.

"Yes," she said smiling, patting my short curls, "the mountains of Austria."

"Have you been there?" I asked.

"Oh, yes." She smiled.

"Are there green lakes in those mountains?"

"Yes," she said, "just the color of your dress."

The presence of Frederick came to me so strongly that I smelled the ambergris of our lovemaking. Michael was talking to his mother and father, who sat at a little round table near the dance floor. His hair was shiny black like the wings of a raven and he was smiling. The younger town girls always smiled and giggled when he passed and any of the local girls would have fought me for him. Still, in my weakest self, which was the strongest part of me, I loved Frederick. The dense veil of sky outside seeped inside and like the weather from the death of a loved one, it would take forever to pass.

For years, I thought of Frederick's paintings of me: a child's face upon a woman's body and the reverse. Once he even painted my head on the sleeping body of Sheila, which I found both amusing and unsettling. Still, his paintings were alive, more alive than the girl posing on the sheep's wool in the dungeon or the girl listening to her parents bicker, or the one watching the sea and longing for her sister, or even the married one having child after child.

These painting memories made an island of me, kept Michael from getting too close, but something happened after our second son was born. Our older son, Dana, who was three at the time, stood admiring the new baby boy in my arms, then asked, "How many days before he'll open his eyes?"

Michael and I knew he was making reference to the kittens that were constantly being born to the cats that took refuge in the shed. It made us smile at one another, and in Michael's eyes I saw the love he had for Dana, and the love for me, too. So, the painting memories began to dissipate, making me regret the time I spent thinking of them and of Frederick's wild and unrestrained love — so rough at times that it was a punishment. The kind of love that made his baby — our coydog — small and sickly and premature, a baby that brought Bertie to tears when she saw it.

The baby's filmy coating seemed to be all that held her together. How could she have been anything but small and sickly? I had barely eaten. I had almost drowned in a sleep of longing: longing to be painted, to be rescued by Frederick. Surely, it is a sin to love a man so much that you deny your own child. Maybe that was the devastating love Mother warned me against.

Beneath the baby's filmy afterbirth, lanugo the color of wheat fields covered her small back. Bertie washed the baby and patted that lanugo down, then dressed her in a white flannel gown and laid her at my breasts. The baby turned her sallow face away as if she didn't know me, when all the time it was I that didn't know her. I had not thought of her, had not pictured her nor imagined holding or bathing or dressing her. She was the growing place created by a man's leaving, the hollow place where I suppose sins against the child can begin.

Only days before the baby was born, she rolled inside me and the shape of a tiny foot pressed out the side of my belly. It was shocking. A foot. A baby's foot. Inside me. How can a baby live inside of nothing? I showed it to Michael and he rubbed her foot, warmed it through my belly with the palm of his hand. Only then did the baby feel welcome, only then would she begin her descent into this world, into the arms of a family with whom she had no true relation.

Michael named her Dorie. After my mother, he said, but perhaps it was after one of the small boats tethered to the shore. The ones that often turned upside down in a storm, but never sank. After she was born, my breasts filled with milk she would not take. My nightie soaked through until Bertie taught me to express the milk, to milk myself, massaging and squeezing the clear sweet liquid into a round glass bowl. Then Bertie bottled it and fed it to the sickly baby, rocking and humming those high and crucial notes beside the kitchen stove, while I slept in the room above or went to the library, whiling the afternoons away. *Sweet sixteen.*

Bertie MacDonald bolstered Dorie with her soily strength and lullabies and her cooing filled in where my love should have been taking root. I was misplaced among the MacDonalds. They were so patient and loving. Never any arguing or unkindness spoken, no doors slamming or rooms filled with chilly resentment. Once, after my parents had a fight, I asked my mother why she let Father be mean to her. She was curled on her bed, her silver tears making a puddle on the pillow. "Life is what you get used to," she said.

Michael and I did not consummate our marriage until three months after Dorie was born. Although he tried, I always turned away, still feeling as if I would be cheating. I also knew Catholic law well enough to know that an unconsummated marriage was not considered legal. I was born to a Catholic father and often attended Mass with him as a child. If Frederick returned, I could have my marriage annulled. In sleep, Frederick's deep guttural voice caressed me. Often Michael shook me from a sweating dream, making me furious because he had taken me from Frederick, plucked me from desire. I know now much of this desire was ignited by being pregnant. Four pregnancies taught me the increased blood supply can heighten things in many ways: Your tongue wants foods in their purest state: oranges, grapes and melons. You thirst for clear water. Your cheeks and body fill with a heat that tingles and burns within you steadier than any fire. Your sleep is as deep as a canyon and your legs open willingly, your canyon cracking deeper until the unborn child carves its way through you.

156

Once, it occurred to me that maybe at the very time a woman is pregnant and the most womanly she can be, perhaps she is also the most manly, freed by her body's fire. *Desire.* It made me long for Frederick. He would study me and find my changing body compelling — something to sketch, to enjoy. He would not blush as Michael did when he found me lounging naked on our bed.

Still, Michael was a kind and caring man, a rocky side hill of ever-blooming cosmos — the ones that seed themselves year after year. And eventually I'd love Michael, but the memories of Frederick remained: him sketching my naked body or watching the words come from my mouth, as if they were great seabirds caught between us in a downdraft. Him, looking at me, through me, touching me like a man who'd touched a million women but at that moment only wanted one. Him, circling, caressing so timely, so expertly coaxing my crescendo: *Good girl. You are my good girl.*

Bertie said once that a child who doesn't hear the high notes of a parent's playful voice will not develop as much confidence as those who do. I didn't remember a playfulness in my parents' voices, but for a time, Frederick had built me up with his playful whisperings, his breath and tongue shaping me like a castle from sand. When you look at one, is it not hard to believe that soon it will be washed away? Its moats and turrets, lookouts and drawbridges gone.

Sometimes I left Dorie with Bertie and went back to my old home, dragging myself up the side hill. Only when I stepped inside the cold and airless house did I realize Mother was really gone, buried up on that abandoned hill with the sailors of foreign waters. Sometimes, I dreamed of her pulling the sailors from their graves and running with them playfully. She seemed so herself and alive, the way she was at the skating pond. One morning remnants of this dream convinced me Mother must be at home. She couldn't possibly be dead, for in the dream I smelled the sweet honey of her neck. I wrapped Dorie snugly. Bertie said the baby was wrapped too tightly and, of course, she was. It wasn't intentional, but a mother who is not in the habit of mothering will always overwrap or underwrap, overfeed or underfeed, overlove or underlove.

For the first time, though, I ignored Bertie's advice and took my mummychild with me. When I couldn't find Mother, I lit a fire in the kitchen stove and snuggled in front of it with the baby to wait, sinking into a dream that was a series of memories: Mother, being hit with the puck; Father, painting my mother's damaged face; me, burning my skates in the stove, the dream so real that the smell of burning leather filled it.

Michael found us asleep, beneath a haze of smoke, because I hadn't remembered to open the flue. When he pulled me up, repeating my name, I was dreaming of a newborn wearing a white gown.

He rushed us from the house, squeezing my arm and saying, "What are you thinking, Elizabeth?"

The distant spruces were as black as soot against a magenta sky. Lights were brightening in the houses. Michael told me to wait. He pointed his finger and said, "Wait," then rushed back inside only to reappear moments later with a sweater. It was one Mother had knit for me from an illustration in Robert McCloskey's book *Time of Wonder.* For some reason, she had chosen the illustration of the mother and daughter sailing to put on the front of the sweater. I remembered the words from that page:

And then at sunset, with porpoises puffing and playing around your boat, you come about and set a course for the island that is home.

Mother used to say that someday she'd get us a little sailboat. Maybe that was why she chose to knit that scene. It was her way of pledging a shared future with me, a way of getting used to her life and helping me get used to mine. In the illustration, the mother is holding the mainsail while the daughter is letting out the jib. Without the jib, the boat is likely to turn into the wind. Maybe Mother sometimes thought of me as the one who steadied her course. I know now that if you allow them, that is exactly what children can do.

Michael lifted Dorie from my arms and loosened her blankets. She rolled into the crook of his arm. I put the sweater on and he led me home, but said nothing. A sliver of moon was coming up over the bay: a baby's thin and slender fingernail. Beneath it floated ghostly fishing boats. The night was brisk and damp as only sea villages can be. I did not want to follow Michael. Maybe women never settle into their husbands, maybe a man feels more like a hotel than a home. Maybe it is the home of origin that lives the strongest in her mind. Surely, it did for my French grandmother and for my mother, too.

Bertie and Mr. MacDonald had eaten their supper, but ours was waiting on the back of the woodstove — roast beef hash in the black frying pan: potatoes, sweet onions and turnip. It would be one of the last winter meals. Even in the dank night, spring was now a waking sour scent and soon Bertie would be gathering the rhubarb, the fresh fiddleheads and beet greens and asparagus. Seasons in and seasons out, she harvested what she could from the land to care for us, just as Michael and his father harvested the sea.

That night, I dreamed of the white-gowned baby again, picking the dream up like a knitting stitch that had been dropped. She seemed a warning. When I woke, Michael was kissing me. His hand snaked into my panties and he rubbed between my legs until I was warm and moist, then climbed on top of me and pushed inside. Dorie had changed my interior, some parts loose, some parts tight, but Michael persisted until we both smelled warm and earthy. His skin was oily as if he'd just been running. At our bedroom window, a fire seemed to flame in the distance, but we were both too close to love's undertow to pull away. There is nothing as compelling as waking to lovemaking; you are still floating in your subconscious, which is neither accusing nor judging. It has no memory or future. It is simply a state and all desires within it are natural, desires that might otherwise seem unrestrained. I suppose it is the most animal one can be and while Michael hovered over me I remembered the girl with the dog's body in Frederick's painting, that beast and girl, that other man's creation, and suddenly I was not at all passive, but began to move in agreement with Michael, setting my mind on the day he car-

161

ried me to his bed, in through the back room where the cream separator sat and even though it was shiny clean, the houseflies buzzed about its lingering tang, into the kitchen and past the warm woodstove and through the living room, squeezing by the closed and dusty piano and up the narrow stairs to his bedroom in the eaves.

Michael's mattress was lumpy yet soft, and the sheets smelled of a day out sailing. I sank into his bed as if to hide in a haystack. Later, I'd wake and watch Mr. MacDonald and Michael lead sixteen black and white cows to the dock and onto a large barge. Each cow resisted the barge as if it were being taken to a slaughter, but they were only being taken out to one of the islands to graze for the summer. I wondered if the sharp smell of them would leave also or if it would simply paddle the air about us until the cows returned in the fall. It is in the memory of the barge pulling away from the dock that I surrendered to Michael, silently, to the feeling of warm sun on my face and smooth, smooth gliding beneath.

In years to come, Michael and I would take our children to the lily pond to skate. One particular night the temperature dropped so fast that the ice froze instantly, sealing the weeds like reaching hands beneath it. Stepping onto the ice in the moonlight took a great deal of faith, because the ice was so transparent, just a congregation of weedy hands waiting to receive you. That first night Michael made love to me, his callused hands received me gently, guided me onto the beautiful smooth blackness and stayed.

2

The flickering at our bedroom window that night was my home burning. Seeing the flames, I tried to run, but Michael wrapped his arms around me tightly. Men were running about the house with pails of water, but the timbers were now visible, collapsing in on themselves like matchsticks. I imagined my family's belongings melting, scenes from a hundred skating sweaters melting, abandoned paint brushes melting, Gwen's Ship of Dreams quilt melting. All the books I hadn't yet retrieved, melting.

"It's for the best," Michael said softly.

"Why would you ever say that? That's my home."

He held me tighter. I began to fight, but it was no use, his arms were like sargassum. "This is your home," he said.

Through tears, the walls fell, the blackened staircase leaned like the mast of a ship, then crumbled. I tried to pull away, but couldn't. "I hate you," I cried.

"I know."

The next day, I noticed Michael's rubber boots behind the woodstove. They were covered in the black oily mud of ashes. It came to me clearly. Of course, Michael couldn't have me running up to the old house looking for Mother, taking Dorie, lighting fires that threatened to injure or kill us both. No loyal husband would allow it.

Bertie rocked and fed the baby while I stood staring at the muddy rubbers. Suddenly, I fell in a heap on the floor, crumbled like the staircase of my home and cried.

"Sssh, sssh," Bertie said, and for the longest time I thought she was hushing the baby until I realized the baby was sleeping. She was hushing me. Hushing me into her world.

"How could he do this to me, Bertie? How could he be so selfish?"

"Sssh, Elizabeth, I want to tell you something. Now listen."

I knew by the sound of Bertie's laden voice that it was something I wouldn't want to hear, words so heavy they can drain into one's heart and rot the sills. Bertie pressed Dorie snugly against her breasts, shoring herself up with the baby, continuing to rock. The slow creaking of the chair would accompany Bertie's story until its end:

"Take your hands away from your ears, Elizabeth. Listen: I was picking crab. The fishing had not been good and we had the twins then, Courtney and Jacob. Do you remember? Did your mother ever tell you?"

I shook my head no.

"No, I expect not. It was something most

165

didn't talk about. Oh, people did for a while after the accident, but then no one knows what to say to you anymore. What more can a person say than sorry? It's as final as we ever get with each other. The twins had just turned three, and it was a blistering hot summer and you know how hot this kitchen can be. Mr. MacDonald had been doing his best, but the truth of the matter was the lobstering hadn't been good and we needed money. I needed to get the crab picked and I just couldn't get it done with the twins in the house. Of course, Mr. MacDonald never picked crab. It's a woman's job. Back then a lot of women picked crab in their homes. Everyone needed the extra. No one does it any more because of regulations. It seems that our homes aren't considered to be clean enough. Well, the twins were busy that day and into everything, so Mr. MacDonald offered to take them out to one of the islands to pick some strawberries. I was fretting about all the canning and preserves I still hadn't done and this was a way for Mr. MacDonald to entertain them and help me at the same time. It was a lovely day and Michael was just six, but a responsible boy, and he, like the twins, deserved a day of being cool on the boat."

Bertie was smiling softly as if watching her family happily walk away from her, a smile made up of satisfaction and longing, a smile that neatly divides a woman's heart forever.

"Anyway," she continued, "Michael was waiting on the dock with the twins while Mr. MacDonald rowed out to get the life jackets from the boat. The tide was in and it had brought in some starfish that were clinging to the pilings beneath the dock. Courtney and Jacob loved to touch them, any child does. They were stretched out on their stomachs on the dock so they could reach into the water. Michael pulled a starfish up that had lost one of its legs and gave it to Courtney and right off, Jacob wanted it and started wrestling her for it. Naturally Courtney pulled away and ran up the dock, calling for me. I was the one that usually worked things out. Michael went after her and when he finally retrieved her and they were on their way back to the dock, he noticed Jacob wasn't anywhere in sight. He called out to him, then rushed right down to the dock and dove in. You know how the water is so deep when the tide is in and it can be dark, black really. Michael kept going to the bottom, but he couldn't find Jacob. Finally, he was beneath the water searching when his father's dinghy made a shadow above him. He rushed to the top to tell him, but before he could dive back down, his father asked him where Courtney was. Michael looked on the dock where he'd seen her last and this is what he told me about that moment. He said,

'Mother, I couldn't face that she might be in the water, too, so I told Dad she'd gone back home with you. I thought if I told him that, it would be true.'"

Bertie lowered her eyes, still slowly rocking. She appeared to be gathering her thoughts, but maybe she was gathering strength from Dorie. She held the baby closer and smelled her head before continuing, "It was an hour or so before they found them. They'd both gotten stuck underneath the dock. We're not sure if they drowned together or if maybe Courtney discovered Jacob already gone. Twins are like that, they have a sixth sense, you know. When they finally found them, Jacob was holding onto the starfish with the missing leg. We like to think that Courtney put it in his hand."

Bertie sighed. "Mr. MacDonald and I have always tried to teach our children to think of the needs of others. Funny thing, we taught them that as a way of survival. It was a way of them getting their minds off themselves. We never thought it would take them away from us." Bertie fell so silent then that I couldn't hear nor see her breathing. After a while, she said solemnly, "The lesson of thinking of others has not been good for Michael. Especially since the drownings. Of course, he blames himself. And when that puck hit your mother, we thought it would be the end of him. He'd been going to the

168

pond for a few years skating and playing hockey and he loved it. It seemed to be the only fun he'd allowed himself since the drownings. His guilt made an awful worker out of him. We thought him shooting that puck and injuring your mother was the last straw. He didn't say much anymore, just did his chores and went up to his room. Then, your mother died. She died. Three deaths he's blaming himself for now. Ever since he's been six years old, his whole life has been spent making up. Doing everything he can for everyone. And not one of those deaths was his fault; they were just bad luck."

Bertie took in a long awkward breath, looking my way, her brows kneeling over her eyes: "I want you to know something, Elizabeth, and I want you to remember it. Michael hasn't got it in him to be selfish. And no one, not even you, will ever know if he needs anything, because he won't let you know and as much as you try, Michael won't really let you love him, because he doesn't think he deserves it."

I tried to make some promise with my face, searching for an expression of understanding, but of course I didn't have one. Those expressions are earned by mothers who have lost. My expression must have been one of not understanding because Bertie continued: "You see, life has made a hole in Michael's heart. And no matter what you pour in, Elizabeth, it's gonna leak out."

I thought of the night before waking to Michael loving me. He was not stealing love. It was not a punishment. He was forceful yet accommodating, and it was for me, somehow, a place of necessity in which he was taking me. Just like the cows, he was delivering me to a place in which I could be provided for — an escape from the burning home. When I arrived at that place that was exactly like an island warmed by the sun, he whispered he'd never leave. I thought back to the dog painting of me. It is said when mating, the female dog remains willing but passive. The cloak of sleep had allowed me to begin in passivity, but then I planted my feet firmly on Michael's bed and opened beneath him. Now, I was committed. I was accountable.

Bertie was looking downward, her tears dropping on the baby's hands like rain. I pictured Bertie's precious twins.

"How did you ever get over them?" I asked.

Bertie looked up, her face the pink of my baby's lips. "You don't," she said. "Death is not something anyone recovers from. You know that. Time is a lot of things, but it is no healer."

Just then, I wanted to hold Dorie, really hold her, squeeze her, kiss her, lick her, but I didn't dare take her from Bertie's arms. Not now. Instead, I told Bertie about my dream of the white-gowned baby I'd had the night before. I told her how it lay so still in the dream. When I did, the pink slipped from Bertie's face and her lips went as slack as rubber bands.

"Are you all right, Bertie?"

"Elizabeth," she said, "do you know what a woman fears most about another woman?"

"No," I admitted, "I don't."

"Her intuition," Bertie said, placing Dorie on her shoulder and rubbing her back. "The night before my twins drowned, I had the sweetest dream of them playing in our church. I could hear their voices and laughter just like they were in Sunday School, but when I tried to open the church door, it was locked. I called for them, but they just kept on laughing and playing like my voice meant nothing to them."

"How do you stand remembering, Bertie?"

Bertie smiled. "I can stand my own sadness. It's the shared sorrows that do you in."

I pictured a family's sorrow as a tall white fence that would always keep them corralled together. Forever islanders.

Dorie rolled her face toward Bertie and Bertie kissed her forehead. With her lips near my baby's head, she told me how she and Mr. MacDonald and Michael had gone down to the dock the night the children drowned. The hearse had come and taken the twins to

171

the funeral home, but they still couldn't believe what had happened.

"The house was awful without them. I don't know what we were thinking, but I have a feeling we all believed maybe it wasn't true. Maybe it had just been a bad dream. You know, there's a time when death is still so close that you think you might have another chance. You might be able to win against it. If you can just manage to stop time for one second, you'll be able to undo things. And you'll go over and over everything in your mind looking for that loophole. Anyway, we walked down to the dock. The sun was setting and all the harbor was purple and it was still awful hot. The gulls even seemed to be too hot to caw and they were whining, swooping over the shore and whining. Since then, I've always believed nature mourns with us. I remember thinking that's what my heart's doing, it's just whining for my babies. We were all walking close enough to each other to touch, but I'm sure we were thinking our own thoughts until we got down there on the dock. It rocked a little beneath us, so we just stood still looking out and I don't know who saw them first, but I know we all saw them. The twins' life jackets were lying in the dinghy. Just the way they lay, you could see Courtney and Jacob in them, the orange ties around their little bodies, sleeping the way they'd sleep after a day out to one of the islands. We all cried, hung on to each other just as if we were drowning, too, and cried." Bertie wiped at her tears with her injured hand. Her missing fingers were never more noticeable than when she cried. Finally, she got up and passed me the baby. Dorie had fallen back to sleep and her dark hair and face were damp where she lay against Bertie. "Some are blown apart by tragedy, Elizabeth, and some are glued together. It's a choice."

I carried Dorie outside. A warm wind was blowing from the west, which generally meant the weather would remain fair and good for fishing. Michael was piling lobster traps in the side yard. I sat down on the cool grass and watched him. The sun was warm for May and the air still smelled of smoke. Not only had my home burned the night before, but in the evenings, islanders were setting fire to their lawns and fields, so they would grow greener in the summer months to come. All of Stonington was a smoldering hill.

Michael had taken his shirt off. Lately, he'd been diving for sea urchins because the Japanese considered them a delicacy and were paying a high price. His body was lean and taut; his back as straight as a lupine stalk. Already he had a fisherman's tan: dark arms and a glistening milky chest with two thin lines of hair in the shape of a black cross. Every once in a while, he looked over at me and said — *What* — smiling the smile of a couple's secrets, but I was not thinking of our lovemaking just then, I was thinking of Michael and his loyalty. It occurred to me that maybe he didn't even love me when all the time I was just taking it for granted, thinking I was the one who must find it in myself to love him. Me, the liar, the one with the bastard child, the one choosing the dreams of a long-gone lover over the ever-present body of someone who had even in his childhood been an honorable man.

When the lobster traps were piled, he came and sat beside me. There was a line of bubbly sweat along his upper lip. I put my face on his bare shoulder and smelled the bitter of his underarms. Dorie was beginning to stir and she cooed, making my milk let down. I started to get up, but Michael pulled me toward him. He brushed my cheek with his warm brown fingers, then unbuttoned my white blouse and touched my wet raisin nipple.

"Feed her yourself, Elizabeth."

In the warm sun, Michael's eyes had turned the bright grassy green of the summer fields to come. I was afraid of Dorie rejecting me, but still I put her to my breast and her warm lips instantly latched on. Michael watched her suckle and smiled. Suddenly, I knew it was the least and the most I could do for him: Love someone he loved.

Dorie looked up, watching my face. For the first time, I took in her round blue eyes and button nose, her fleecy, downy brown hair like a cap and her skin that mirrored the prettiest pink of Bertie's. It is said that the distance between a mother's face and a child nursing at her breast is the distance in which the baby first begins to see. Of course, Dorie was five months old, so she had been seeing for quite some time the gentle face of Bertie MacDonald feeding her from a bottle, but I had not been seeing. Maybe the distance between a mother's face and her baby might be when some mothers first begin to see. Bertie's words came back: *Some are blown apart by tragedy and some are glued together.*

With Dorie sucking and Michael's arm around me, we seemed to make a sort of love together, the three of us. I suppose it's not that uncommon, the lovemaking of family, but for me, it was a world I'd never even imagined, a comfort made up of bodies and feelings and sucking sounds, of past and present and future, tattered fabric sewn so lovingly back together that no amount of scrutiny could reveal its stitching.

Michael put his hand in front of Dorie. She wrapped her tiny fingers around one of his. He watched her closely as did I, realizing for the first time that not only was I her mother, but he, Michael, was her father.

3

I had fantasies of my father calling and of the two of us being reunited, but the memory of him naked with my mother would be his last and final scene. I would, however, eventually stand in front of one of his paintings at an art gallery on Newbury Street in Boston and be overcome with such mourning as to truly understand my sister's words that *mourning is wishing.* I wished for him. In a way, I'd never wished for another. The painting was of a winged bull carrying three women on its back across the night sky. Starless, moonless, a night like soot upon a raven's wings. In it, I saw the black infinity of family, the silt that gathers in the veins of each of us until we are unrecognizable even to ourselves. In this night painting, all Father's usual distracting details had disappeared. The sinewy black strength of the bull's wings seemed an irrepressible desire to rescue. If ever a painting showed the potential of a man's love, this was it. I looked to the painting's title card and there the necessary word stood printed beneath my father's name:

Peter Earl Johnson
Master

The art gallery had to painstakingly clean Father's painting *Master* after acquiring it. The great bull with three women on its back was covered with Father's dried blood. After completing it, Father shot himself between his eyes, the very place Mother had sustained her injury. This, I suppose, was their shared sorrow, and perhaps you could call his choice of injury a symbol of empathy or maybe even love or, although I hate to think it, of competition. Actions and feelings may take the form of clouds, but they are not as easy to figure out.

There was a second painting of Father's called *Traveling*. In it, an old couple were sitting close together in a car coming toward the viewer, a night sky of stars behind them, with a look of anticipation on each of their faces. A brilliant light shone up from the dash making the couple glow, but also bleaching their features somehow. Still, it was clearly the older faces of my parents and it was the look that Father often had while painting or Mother had while skating, but it was not a look I'd ever seen them share. It was a look of longing and in the painting they weren't quite sharing it either. They stared ahead intently. Maybe this was as close as they could be. I kept trying to see if Gwen and I might have been painted in the backseat, but it was completely dark with not even a wavy shadow to suggest someone else's presence.

A scrawled note came from Celise informing me of Father's suicide and telling me he blamed himself for my mother's death. She'd taken care of the cremation and burial. Celise said Father was buried across the river from Boston in the same cemetery as Winslow Homer. Who was Winslow Homer and how many cemeteries were across the river from Boston? My father had disappeared like the bone that cracked, then dissolved in my mother's face — with no way to find or restore it. Sometimes at night, I dreamed of walking through darkened cemeteries. Later, when I confessed this to Bertie, she said, "We all deserve to bury our loved ones." She said, "The time between a loved one's death and burial is possibly the hardest. You wonder where they are and how they are being handled. One thing is sure, Elizabeth, they are being handled by hands unfamiliar with your loved one's body. They have not watched them or known them to move through life as you have." Bertie paused, seeming to catch her breath. "But no matter what, we have the dance of them in us, Elizabeth. No one can take that away, not even death."

I saw my mother skating and my father sketching beside the lily pond. These were the things that determined their identity, their very essence, and Bertie was right, their

dance had stayed with me, lingering like per-
fume after a party.

The feeling I had while reading Celise's
letter was *stratus:* a low, quiet uniform sheet
like fog. Dull gray stratus clouds often make
a heavy, leaden sky in which only fine drizzle
falls. So few tears fell from that cloud. I
hung on to them until larger, more ominous
clouds came my way.

4

On the night that Michael and I consummated our marriage, we made a baby, a beautiful round girl that we would watch closely the same way we watched Dorie nurse for the first time, but she, our second child, would be our first shared sorrow. Even though I thought of her each day she grew inside of me and ate and slept and prepared for her in a caring mother's way, thanks to Bertie's instruction, even so, she would not come to us complete.

For one perfect snowy day, we admired our baby's big and lovely face, her fat and wrinkled body, her closely tucked ears, her tuft of dark hair, trying to choose a name, only to have her die the next night while sleeping between us. We thought we'd smothered her. She looked in death like the healthiest child ever born. Her lips were even curled and smiling.

The doctor told us after examining her it was not our fault and that is where we left her, in Blue Hill on the doctor's examining table, a blank white sheet of crinkly paper beneath her; a life that would never be drawn. Leaving my baby there alone is one of my biggest regrets. Now, I would do it differently. I would hold her longer, just as I would hold my dead mother longer if I could.

The next day, our baby was delivered to the cemetery vault, still unnamed. It was February and the earth was frozen. Later, the doctor called to say tests had shown the baby was born with a hole in her heart. He said, "Elizabeth, no amount of love or care could have saved her." I thought how our little girl took on her father's damaged heart — the figurative translating into the literal. And then, as if a bank of endless fog had lifted, revealing a precious landscape — the landscape being my broken-hearted husband — I began to love Michael.

From our bedroom window, I watched him coming up from the dock. An ice storm had come in the night before. All the island was sparkling in sunlight. Limbs bowed down and gleamed, and some of the telephone poles were leaning over with ice-laden wires. The roads were a sheet of ice; there would be no leaving the island. Once during an ice storm, Mother put her skates on and skated up and down Main Street. People went to their windows to watch her. I must have been smiling remembering her, because when I looked down at Michael, he had stopped and was smiling up at me. His smile seemed painted on his face though, and I knew like the ice all around us, it could be as destructive as it was beautiful. His pretending. How many deaths can a man carry? My father hadn't managed to carry one.

When Michael came up the stairs and I told him about our little girl's heart, he curled up on the bed and wept.

Later, when he was looking off, lonely, toward the dock, I simply whispered, "We'll make another."

"It won't be the same," he said.

"Of course not, but it will be a comfort."

We did make another and another, two boys after the little girl still unnamed and buried beside my mother. Even now, I picture my white-gowned baby skating with Mother and when I look back I know it was the baby I was dreaming of the night she was conceived, the night my home burned. It was intuition.

In icy winters to come, Michael taught the children to skate and me as well, holding my stiff elbow and steadying me across the lily pond. I'd forgotten everything and it was so important to Michael that I learn to skate again, that I not just sit and watch like most of the mothers. I loved the sound of my blades scratching across the fresh ice, the sight of children pushing a chair in front of them, twirling and falling, laughing and standing up, rebounding. I loved the fire's woodsy smell in the skating shed, and when I got back home I loved the tired ache in my legs. *I was alive.*

Soon, I took the children to the pond myself, packing peanut butter and jelly sandwiches, Bertie's sugar cookies and a Thermos of cocoa. While we walked toward the pond, I felt myself as my mother, tall and statuesque, strong and determined. The children ran ahead, their skates resting over their shoulders, and I knew without a doubt they were leading me, steadying my course. They were my jib.

In later summers, strawberries grew on the hill where my home used to be, and often I took the children there, too. I loved the way the berries stained their tiny fingers and how later their bath water would turn pink when the stains washed away, the very pink of my mother's deathly tear. Maybe intuition can show itself on a mother's face. Maybe my mother was leaving a sign for me, a sign of sad times turning beautiful.

The skating pond in the winter and my home field in the summer became a comfort. I could go to these places and return to my past, remembering my parents and my life the way it once was. Ice could melt, homes could burn, loved ones could die, but the earth remained. And I could be on that earth, alive, just as my parents were before they left it.

I was picking late strawberries in my home field when Frederick's hand came down on mine, so wrinkled and old, the blue veins permanently etched above the skin like streams. "Elizabeth?"

Before I dared to look up, he said my name again: *Elizabeth.*

I stood, dropping a handful of berries to the ground, then looked to see his weathered face. My children gathered around me. Dorie, who was twelve at the time and always so happy to meet a stranger, looked questioningly at Frederick. Did she see the resemblance? The mellow skin. The square jaw. The long lean body and lonesome gray eyes. I took her hand, trying to lead her behind me, but she peered at him curiously.

I tried to say hello, but couldn't.

Frederick smiled, his teeth just as white as they were so long ago. He looked at each of my children, which prompted me to send them home with the strawberries, assuring them I'd follow along soon. They kept glancing back and checking until they disappeared beneath the hill.

Frederick's smile was as attractive as ever, framed by deeper lines now. Crevices I could fall into. "You're blushing," he said, watching me, watching him. "I know," he said, "you're thinking how old I've become."

There was a camera around his neck. He tipped the lens up and stared into it.

"Frederick, what brings you here?"

"I wanted to take some pictures."

"Oh," I said, slightly disappointed that it didn't have something to do with me. He reached out and touched my hair that was floating in the sunlight. Much longer now than he'd ever seen it, trailing in sun-stained ringlets below my waist. Immediately, he captured me in his essence, his confident movements, his beautiful hands, his soapy smell, his smile. While touching my hair, he seemed on the verge of saying something.

"Is there something you want, Frederick?"

"Just to see you again," he said.

I looked down, rubbed at the berry stains on my fingers, shifting my weight back and forth. He pulled his hand back, rested it on his hip. "Elizabeth, do you ever leave here? Do you ever leave Stonington?"

"Not often." I smiled. "I don't drive."

He grinned, then looked off to the sea. "Is there a place we could meet to talk?"

I knew I should say no. The earth beneath me suddenly felt jagged and narrow as if I were teetering on a ledge. But of course, I said yes, not knowing the means in which I would travel to meet him.

What does a woman fear most about herself?

Her intuition.
Why?
She knows she should pay attention.
What is my biggest fear?
That I'll be punished for my choices.

Part Four

1

Before Frederick showed up, I spent almost every day that summer lobstering with Michael. Mr. MacDonald had fluid around his heart and was unable to go out to sea. Still, he came down to the dock in the mornings and helped fill the bait bags, then went back to join Bertie who was watching the children. It seemed natural for me to go off with Michael. I always hated being left behind.

Michael had a new boat, a Duffy 35', which he'd christened the *Elizabeth Dorie*. The power of the new boat under me, the way the temperature gradually slid down as we sped out of the harbor, the cleansing fresh smell, the gelid air was exhilarating. Some mornings the bright rising sun spread like a drop of mercury hitting the wide open sea, blinding me to the jagged shore and tiny houses, to the scattering of fishing boats, deafening me to the screeching of the seagulls flying behind us, racing to keep up with the oily scent of mackerel in the bait bags.

Over the summer, the warm sun turned my face the color of chestnuts. Helping to lift the traps had muscled my arms and shoulders and for the first time in many years I felt strong. I was twenty-seven years old, had been married to Michael for almost twelve years, and we were finally dating. Every day we had a set time to meet, a plan to be alone. Without the auspices of work, we never had the confidence to search each other out — we never had the confidence to be anything but lonely. Our gatherings were fumblings in the dark. Whisperings.

Sometimes when we finished pulling the traps, we would anchor the boat in a secret cove where we'd eat the lunch Bertie had packed for us. We devoured the food. If the weather was cool, Bertie packed hefty chicken salad sandwiches or cold roast beef on thick slices of brown bread coated with mustard, or maybe a Thermos of barley soup. If the weather was hot, she packed egg salad with chives from her garden or cucumbers sliced as thinly as paper with dill and mayonnaise, the crust cut away. We nibbled the elegant sandwiches. They were too extravagant to gobble down — sandwiches of gatherings and celebrations. Often, the sweets were special, too. Delicate butter cookies swirled with white icing and a slice of cherry on top. Wedding cookies. Or a hot milk cake with brown sugar icing and coconut.

Michael was at home on the boat, stepping around the coiled lines, scratching his forearm thoughtfully while he steered into open waters, knowing exactly where the shoals and whirlpools hid. Knowing the markers and the tides. His sureness was attractive. Sometimes while finishing our warm tea, he'd massage my feet. We talked of the house we planned to build in the fall. Michael had already purchased two acres across from the lily pond and we'd spent many nights drawing up plans at the kitchen table, the children standing over us and making their own requests. Michael wanted something similar to his parents' house, a cozy Cape in which the children could sleep like squirrels in the eaves. I wanted soaring spaces. We both wanted to look out at the lily pond, to watch the seasons cast it like a series of different paintings. Although we hadn't said it, I think we both wanted to accept the past and see the lily pond for what it was. Alive and beautiful. We'd saved enough money to have the basement dug and soon a crew of men would put up the frame. Michael planned to finish the inside with his father's help over the winter. We were excited but there was also some regret about leaving his parents. I'm sure their feelings, like ours, were mixed. At times, they, too, must have felt crowded, but still they were as attached to the children as the children were to them. And they were such a help to Michael and me. I never could have raised my children without Bertie. Most days, it was I who helped her, assisting here and there while she took on the role of real caregiver. Not just to the children, but to all of us, sometimes spotting our needs before we even felt them in ourselves. The change would take some getting used to for everyone, but I pictured it as a bridge I needed to cross, a necessary pilgrimage to really being a mother and a wife, to growing up. In some ways, this frightened me. What if I failed?

On the boat, Michael and I talked of the children. Dorie's shy and reticent ways, her long legs that made her a natural runner. Her beautiful fingers dancing over the chipped piano keys, an octave the easiest thing in the world for her to reach. Bertie had taught her. Sometimes in the evenings, we had sing-alongs while Dorie played. The neighbors listening must have thought: *Now that's a happy family. Why can't we be like that?*

But lately, Dorie was withdrawn, choosing to be alone in her room, listening to the radio. It was natural, Michael said, but sometimes I wanted to grab her, shake her, insist that she join us. Other times, I just wanted her to be a baby again so we could start over. Maybe her withdrawing was about me. Maybe she was mirroring my own withdrawn and distant nature.

We talked about our sons, Dana and Vincent, who wrestled one another like pups and liked to go crabbing on the dock, the fisherman's tan already imprinted on their boy bodies. Dana was nine, his square teeth jumbled in his mouth, his nose freckled, his eyes the grassy green of Michael's, a blotchy burn scar on his chin where he'd fallen against the woodstove when he was learning to walk. He loved to read, devouring books like cookies. He was a thinker.

Vincent was our showoff. At six, he liked to dress up, put on plays, imitate people. He teased his brother and sister, put plastic mice in their beds, tied their sneaker laces together while they sat at the table. We all spoiled him. We couldn't help but, he was so naturally affectionate and loving. His brown eyes and round wide nose all jutting forward like the face of a harbor seal. Vincent liked to draw. His drawings of his father and grandfather in their boat were so well done — the curve of his grandfather's slumping back, his father's muscled arms and squinting eyes — that we all looked at the pictures from time to time, marvelling at his ability to capture the essence of his loved ones.

From the beginning, Michael took pleasure in our children. They became the marks on his compass and they instructed most of his decisions. He recorded and reveled in all their firsts as did Bertie and Mr. MacDonald: first smile, first grasping, first standing, first crawling, first tooth, first word, first step, first drawing, first song, first fall from their crib, first prayers, first haircut, first outing on the boat . . .

Michael and I didn't share ourselves as much as we shared our love for the children, though. I was still held back, tethered to my past somehow. Once, I was picking over oranges at Bartlett's store when I noticed a man watching me. Not a fisherman, but a sailor. Not a local, but a tourist. He smiled, something of Frederick's easiness in his smile. I squeezed an orange. The word *satsuma* returned.

Walking home with a dozen oranges, I remembered the way Frederick peeled oranges for me, slitting them in sections, and the way he held me firmly when we made love, the smoky hazing of his eyes. Remembering it hazed my own eyes, warmed them like the day around me. It made me want to find the stranger from the market. Maybe his sailboat was anchored in the harbor. Maybe I could row out after dark — let him lift me up over the side — let him be a stranger with me. A lover. Maybe all the feelings I'd reserved for Frederick could be transferred to another. Sealed like a secret in a bottle and pushed out to sea.

On the *Elizabeth Dorie*, I was tempted to confess my restlessness to Michael. Maybe it would be good for him to know that sometimes my life seemed a wilderness — a place I got caught in while on my way somewhere else — a whirlpool, a rocky shoal. If I confessed, my desire might fade in the same way a disturbing dream fades after you tell it. Maybe if Michael knew, he'd use the same strength with me as he used on the lobster boat, he'd tighten my lines to keep me from drifting. I wasn't sure what my confession might do to Michael, though. Only in the last few years had he become comfortable with me. Playful, openly affectionate. Confessing could destroy that, wipe it away like a child's drawing on a steamy window.

When I felt tempted to be truthful, I'd strip down to my bra and panties and sun on the bow of the boat. All my life, I'd watched bikinied women doing this aboard the occasional pleasure boats that came into Stonington harbor. It felt good to claim it as something I could do, too — a fisherman's wife — lie on my stomach, sometimes reading my book or letting the gentle rocking lull me into a nap while Michael neatened the boat and curled lines. Sometimes, when he was finished with his chores, we made love, being daring on the bow or stretched out on the long seat under the bulkhead. Michael always kept a blanket for us on the boat. A red wool blanket, which he lay beneath me like an offering. *Our blanket,* he called it. The wool scratched my back and bottom, left it red and blotchy, made me feel alive. Privacy in the MacDonald house was fleeting, especially with our growing children. It was one of the reasons we couldn't wait for our new house. One thing we agreed on when planning the house was a bedroom door that could lock.

Anchored, we might swim around the boat, diving and rubbing against one another, then floating to the surface. Once while wet and hanging on to a boat line, I asked Michael if he regretted marrying me. He slicked his hair back. "I regret," he teased, "not marrying you sooner."

I slapped his arm. "I was fifteen when you married me."

He pulled me close. "Yes, but you would have made a beautiful child bride."

"I was a child bride," I said, wondering if he still thought I was beautiful.

Michael squinted. "Still," he said, "forever is a very short time." It was a departure from his usual teasing, a slight opening of the door to his broken heart.

Later, speeding back home, both standing at the wheel and watching for Stonington, Michael teased me about being first mate on a loveboat. I teased him back by saying he wouldn't be so cocky when his mother asked what made us so late. He looked at me, smiled, his teeth pearly white between his tanned and blistered lips. My lips reflected in his dark sunglasses and they had a satisfied curve. The very curve on the lips of Father's portrait of me.

From a distance, we'd always see the kids waving from our dock, the large wheelbarrow beside them waiting for the day's catch. Bertie and Mr. MacDonald hovered behind them, standing bravely on the pier of their loss, Sheila faithfully beside them.

My children looked so tiny, their life-jacketed bodies slowly growing as we sped closer. When they weren't wearing them, their life jackets hung beside the back door on hooks. Who knew when the sea might wash in and take someone? It happened in Stonington. The ghosts of the missing walked the shores at night, knocked on closed doors and crept through hallways while we slept.

Bertie and Mr. MacDonald always made the children kneel when we got closer and the dock rocked, reminding me how Bertie knelt to pray each night. Sometimes, I'd glimpse her kneeling at the side of her bed, her long hair braided down her back, her beautiful hand resting on the injured one.

Depending on the wind, the night sounds might be a baby crying, a seagull calling, a screeching cat in heat, or a lone fishing boat motoring in late. Listening, I'd think what a lonely place Stonington was. No wonder the ghosts tried to get close to us. No wonder women prayed.

When we neared the dock, I'd throw the fenders out, then hold the throttle in neutral while Michael jumped out to tie the lines. Dana would shout, "How many *lob'stas* did you get today?"

"More than will fit in that wheelbarrow," Michael might say, or, "Guess and I'll give you a dollar."

If Bertie asked what took us so long, Michael always had a story. "Two porpoises and their baby came to the boat. We fed them your cream cheese sandwiches, Mother. They just loved them. Thought they were at a party. Didn't go for the Whoopie Pies, though . . ." Michael tied the lines, pulling the boat in snugly.

Often, Dorie asked me to take her and the boys for a spin. Unlike the boys, who would have been happy playing around the dock or picking up the clacking lobsters, Dorie always wanted to go out. She already had the itch that island girls get, their eyes not on the horizon, but beyond, their sweet berry lips not yet knowing the prayers that can make women stay.

Sometimes, on Saturdays while Michael worked at his traps, we'd go for a picnic to one of the abandoned islands. The boys would spend the whole day imagining themselves as Robinson Crusoe and Friday while Dorie wandered to the edges of the island searching out unusual plants and berries, or finding shells along the shore, holding them to her ear, listening. In the distance, her singing often floated back to me:

Cape Cod girls they have no combs
Heave away . . . Heave away
They comb their hair with cod fish bones,
We are bound for Australia
Heave away my bully bully boys,
Heave away . . . Heave away
Heave away and don't you make a noise,
We are bound for Australia . . .

In the fall we'd go as far as the Cranberry Islands to pick cranberries in the bogs. On our way, we might see a family of puffins or winter ducks. Once we cut the motor to watch eagles soaring near the high ledge of an island.

"They're birds of prey," Dana my little reader said. He looked up, a worried vertical line between his eyes. "You know what, Mom?"

"What, sweetheart?"

"A long time ago, if you shot one, you got twenty cents."

"Oh, that's awful."

Vincent looked curiously at his older brother. "Why did you get twenty cents?"

" 'Cause those birds were eating the island lambs."

Another time on a tiny shoal, we spotted a stranded seal pup. Its huge liquid brown eyes watched us pleadingly. Dorie wanted to load the pup in the boat and take it back to Stonington, but I said it was best left alone.

"Please, Mom, please."

"No, Dorie."

"Why, Mom? Something will happen to it if we don't."

"Dorie, we'll call the harbor master when we get home. He'll know what to do."

The seal whimpered.

Dorie stamped her foot. "Mom, you know somebody will come along and shoot it before the harbor master gets out here."

As cute as the seals were, they stole bait from traps and most lobstermen didn't like them. Like all children, mine were aware of the injustices to wildlife. They knew that the harbor seals were very intelligent, that they could recognize individual boats that had shot at them in the past and it was said they could even judge rifle range. This ability of the seal challenged the shooter to test his marksmanship. As we were leaving, Dorie started to cry. "That seal is an orphan, Mom."

"Its mother will come back, Dorie."

"Its mother is probably dead."

For the shortest second, looking back, I

saw myself in the shiny charcoal seal. I was just as alone when Michael rescued me.

Most of our ventures onto the islands were happy times. The children discovered whole worlds in a down-lined eider nest or a swallow's nest, which is made of the mother bird's feathers and is as beautiful and delicate as a feather hat. They marvelled at the long-necked cormorants, the yellow-headed gannets and the awkward-flying great blue heron.

Once on a small island, Dana told Vincent that we were standing right under the Atlantic Flyway, that every migrating bird used the sky above us. When we got home, Vincent drew a number of birds flying across the sky, all wearing aviator caps like Snoopy fighting the Red Baron.

I always hoped that getting to know the islands would cure my children of their wanderlust, especially Dorie. Any islander will tell you, the more you're islanded, the less interested you are in going other places. You get woven into an island like a fly in a spider's web. Even when people from Stonington left the point for a few minutes, they said they were *off the rock*. An expression that made me picture them wandering aimlessly in unfamiliar places. I told Dorie about my father dying without any family in Boston, about Gwen, who Dorie knew and loved. How hard her life had been since she left the island. How she'd never found her place anywhere else. I knew I couldn't hold Dorie back forever, but I wanted her to know the dangers of the outside world. Even at twelve, Dorie knew my stories were warnings. "Gosh, Mom, what are you trying to do? Scare me to death?" My father's threatening and paralyzing stories came back, his stern voice, his smoldering eyes. So, I stopped.

2

After Frederick appeared in the strawberry patch, I also stopped lobstering, telling Michael I needed to spend some time with the children before they went back to school. He hired a teenager named Jeb to help him. Jeb had quit school and lolled about, watching television or drifting around the docks. Michael said he wasn't much help, but he was company.

Each morning I washed my hair and rinsed it with some of the cider vinegar Bertie was using to make her fall pickles. The vinegar made my hair shiny. I put on coral lipstick, blotting it with a tissue, then using the stained tissue to blush my tanned cheeks. Instead of pulling my jeans on with one of Michael's shirts, I'd match a sleeveless eyelet blouse with a brightly colored cotton skirt or soft denim shorts with a velvet vest. My closet became its own world, not a place I sleepily stumbled into to dress, but a place I lingered in, touching the fabrics, admiring their colors, matching them boldly together.

I moved about the village with the children, starting with my home field where we nibbled on the last of the strawberries, then along Main Street and the shops, into the library where the children rummaged through the books as if they were Christmas presents. I perused a book on the painter John Marin. I'd signed it out several times before and knew it by heart: how the artist came to Stonington in the 1920s and some say painted his best watercolors. He was drawn to how uncomfortably the little village sat on its rocks, to the lonely fog and rain and to the fleet of white sun-drenched islands in its bay.

After the library, I'd go out to the tip of each pier, slowly, twisting, turning — a beacon. Sometimes, I was careless, letting the children run ahead or fall behind with kids who mingled on the street corners. The streets were narrow and the locals drove too fast. They were used to powerboats, to owning what lay ahead of them. I no longer noticed the roar and downshifting of half-ton trucks. Instead, I lingered with my thoughts of Frederick, conveniently snipping his cruelty away. Memory is always selective. The memory of a black night sea will become iridescent indigo. A boat trip in which your face freezes in the pounding sleet will become one of the most exhilarating days of your life. I was suddenly drawn to my past. It seemed my last chance to go back. To open what was left unopened. To lick the tongue that had sealed it. My feelings for Michael dissipated like dew. *Why?* Michael was physically and soulfully beautiful. He was committed to me. He had never hurt me. He loved our children, but I was drawn to the strong jaw, the definite desires, the burnt-smelling breath, the older face, the harshness.

On the third day of my wanderings, Bertie said, "Elizabeth, why don't you leave the children with me. I miss them."

I was in a sleeveless blue dress, my hair spritzed with water so that each curl glistened. The children were still sleeping. I lowered my eyes knowing right then that maybe a woman could hide her wayward desires from her husband, but she would never be able to hide them from a woman who knew her well. Bertie was at the kitchen table, cutting up vegetables on a wooden board. Bowls of chopped tomatoes and cucumbers and onions circled her. I usually helped Bertie do the fall pickles, a job I loved because of the smells and colors: red tomatoes, the pale, fresh, seedy center of the cucumbers, the stinging white onions. Each vegetable so distinct until you mixed and cooked them. It was surprising how quickly the vibrant vegetables surrendered their colors, making up a new color that wasn't reminiscent of any of them.

Bertie put the knife down. She held her

damaged hand up. "You asked about my missing fingers once."

"Yes, last year when we were doing the pickles. You didn't want to tell me. Remember?" Anxious to search for Frederick, I was hoping she still wouldn't.

"I never told anyone," she said.

"You don't have to tell me, Bertie. It's none of my business."

"I want you to know, Elizabeth. Sit down."

I hesitated, then took the chair opposite her.

She looked down at her damaged hand, rubbing the back of it. She took her time as if by rubbing her hand, she was coaxing the story to appear like a genie in a pot. "I chopped them off," she said abruptly.

The image took my breath away, the severed fingers lying on the table between us.

"I know," she said. "It's awful to imagine. The shocking thing was I didn't feel a thing. It was painless."

"It was?"

"Yes. I'm not recommending it, Elizabeth. That was a very dark time. I'd do things differently now, but I couldn't help myself. I had guilt."

Bertie continued. "Several years after we lost the twins, I watched Michael and his father walk down to the dock to go out lobstering. It was a bright spring day and Michael was walking kind of hunched over. You know, his shoulders were all rounded in and he didn't look like a boy at all. He was just twelve years old and he looked like an old man. Older than his father."

I looked at her curiously.

"Oh," Bertie said, "he doesn't walk that way anymore. Not since you and the children."

"No," I said, hoping the story could end there. "He walks like a king."

Bertie smiled. "When I looked at Michael all hunched over like that, I knew it was his guilt that was caving him in. And I knew he thought of those twins drowning all the time. And I realized, standing at the window, watching Michael and his father, that the twins hadn't crossed my mind in a while. I'd been busying myself with things so I wouldn't have to think of them. Their own mother." Bertie made a fluttering motion with her hands. "The mind can do that. It can wipe things away if you let it. Good things. You see, I hadn't only wiped away the twins, but I'd wiped away Michael and Mr. MacDonald. I'd let myself enter into a kind of fog. A dull place." Bertie looked up quickly as if someone might be calling her from outside, then said evenly, "That's when I chopped my fingers off. I went out to the tree stump where Mr. MacDonald chops his wood and I did it." She held her hand up, turning it, almost admiring the void. "When

I look back, I think I was trying to jolt myself out of the grayness. It was completely
self-centered. I was afraid."

"What were you afraid of, Bertie?"

"Of never feeling again."

We sat very still. The chickadees had already switched to their winter song and the
squirrels were chattering, the blue jays were
making stabbing sounds and the crows
cawed. It was only September, but the song
birds seemed to be gone, so there was
nothing to soften the harsher hollow sounds
of the bigger birds.

A tear slid down Bertie's face. "Elizabeth,"
she said, "it takes work to let go of your
emptiness. You need to keep things in perspective now."

Bertie stood up, wiping the tear away while
moving to the sink where she began to measure out the cider vinegar. Suddenly, I missed
my mother. Maybe it was Bertie using the
word *perspective*. The very thing my father
said I didn't have, reminding me of the day
he angrily drew our house while Mother took
me skating, telling me on the way *to dream.*

The pouring vinegar made the kitchen
bitter-smelling. Sickly. I covered my mouth
and went to the screen door, took a deeper
breath. Already, the air had fall in it. It
smelled of baked leaves, but there was a
moist saltiness riding on it, too, a smell that
floats over deep water. One of the shed cats

was licking at an empty saucer near the step. Bertie's confession disoriented me. Her fingers lay before me. Severed. It seemed so unlike her — to be brutal — even with herself. *Is that what guilt does to women?*

I stared up at the bright sky thinking of the Atlantic Flyway. Soon, all the birds would be migrating. I'd read of hummingbirds being temporarily paralyzed by a sudden temperature drop during fall migration. The article said the birds literally flip and hang upside down in the trees.

"Bertie, what did you tell Mr. MacDonald and Michael about your fingers? How did you explain your missing fingers to them?"

"I told them I had an accident chopping kindling. Of course, you know your father-in-law, he always has lots of kindling chopped ahead, but he didn't ask any questions."

"Why not?"

"Most men want to believe their wives, Elizabeth. They want to think the best of them. It allows us a lot of leeway."

I looked down at my own fingers. They were the youngest part of me. Almost girlish, still stained from picking strawberries. "Do you have phantom pains, Bertie?"

She cleared her throat. "Nothing causes phantom pains like the heart, Elizabeth. Especially the phantom of a child."

One night a few months back, Michael had

taken the children and me around to Eaton's Lobster Pool in the boat. The cozy restaurant hugs a small protected cove on Little Deer Isle. Michael took us every summer, always telling us to order anything and everything we wanted. We always ordered steaks. Eaton's was packed with summer tourists and the children and I enjoyed watching them. They were noticeably different from us. Confident. Loud. But when it came to cracking lobsters, some of them were hopelessly inexperienced.

That night, the tide was low, revealing huge black mussel flats in the cove that reflected the setting pink sky, making the inside of the restaurant pink. Everyone's skin glowed and so for a time we blended in with the tourists somehow, which felt nice. Easy.

The children finished eating before Michael and I did, so we allowed them to go out and throw stones from the pier where we had docked. Michael and I took our time. He ordered a second serving of coleslaw while I had the strawberry rhubarb pie.

When we were walking back to the boat, I noticed only Vincent and Dorie on the dock. "Where's your brother?" I called out.

They looked to us, then all around. Dorie knelt down and picked up Dana's sneakers, held them up like two hooked fish, then shrugged her shoulders. The tide had come in and covered the flats. The harbor was a smooth pink pool of seawater, gently rising up and down like a heartbeat. Michael hurried out on the dock. Climbed down the ladder. I began hollering Dana's name. It was only a matter of seconds before he answered. He'd gone up near the woods and was picking blackberries and eating them. It was easy to see him once he waved, but the feeling of losing him didn't fade. The very shape of him had ripped through me. I looked back to see Michael clinging to the ladder. Even in the pink light, he was pale, his mouth hanging open. I knew in a matter of seconds, the shape of Dana had ripped through Michael, too. Our little boy already ghostly within us. A hollow, hollow shape.

By the time we got back to Stonington Harbor, the sun had set and the lights were coming up in the houses. The *Elizabeth Dorie* steadily streamed through the water. The children were in their lifejackets near the wheel, watching for markers. Michael was quietly steering. He hadn't said anything, but all the way home, we both kept looking at Dana, kept checking to see if he was really there. The blackberry stains on his mouth helped — they made him very human, but they were also bruisy and deathlike.

"Red right return," Dana said when he saw the red marker. It was a saying Michael had taught the children so they could find their way home on the water. He told them repetition was the key to learning anything. At the time, I couldn't help wondering if it was the way Michael learned to love me. Simply by repeating. Vincent and Dorie joined in, *Red right return,* then I did and finally Michael, each of us chanting our way back home.

Upstairs, one of the children got up and walked down the hallway to the bathroom. It was Dorie. Her step was lighter, quicker than the boys, easily recognized as the steps of a girl her age. I took in a breath. "I'll be back in a little bit, Bertie."

"All right, de-ah," she said solemnly.

"Bertie?"

"Yes."

"What do you do with your guilt?"

"I pray," she said.

If only I had touched the womblike flesh of my children's faces or measured my cheating thoughts against their innocent smiles. If only I'd thought of their hearts aching from a loved one being lost. Instead, I left them in their beds to look for Frederick as casually as one wakes and leaves a pleasant dream behind. If only I'd thought of Michael. Remembered the day he told me he was going to marry me. How worried he was about me being unwed and pregnant. "Who cares, Michael? Nobody cares about me."

"I care," he said.

"But this isn't your baby."

214

"Nobody will know that but us."

"People aren't stupid, Michael. They'll figure it out."

He took me in his arms, smoothed my hair while he held me. "A marriage is a marriage, Elizabeth, no matter what people say. Let me marry you."

I was admiring a piece of granite in the museum window when Frederick came and stood beside me whispering, "Where should we meet?"

In the night, I'd decided on the cemetery. I could trust myself there. When I told Frederick, he looked confused.

"It's peaceful," I said.

He slipped away, dressed in blue jeans, tennis shoes and a beige safari jacket as if this little point of land, this end of the road, this island were his adventure. Everything around him began to sway, the sidewalk, the buildings, a slow-moving car, children passing on their bikes. Even my body swayed inside and out. All the world became a Marin painting. He believed the world was alive, buildings no less than people. Nature was alive with movement, forces, the influence of one mass upon another. I looked back at the pink sparkling granite, so solid and fierce in its beauty. It swayed, too.

At the cemetery, Frederick took my hand

and led me a few steps into the trees where we sat down, he against a cedar tree and I Indian-style near him. There were hundreds of pinecones, which I began collecting in my blue dress. About the village, there were hundreds of apples on the trees, bushes laden with bloated blueberries, rose hips as big as plums, chestnuts and acorns covering the sidewalks and narrow roads; a sign, according to Mr. MacDonald, of a cold and unforgiving winter coming our way.

"You look beautiful," Frederick said. "You haven't changed, have you?"

"I don't know. I never thought about it."

He smiled. "How are you?"

"Good."

"Elizabeth." He touched the back of his hand to my cheek. "There's so much to say to you. I'm not sure where to begin."

My heart pounded in my throat. He lifted my chin so we were eye to eye. "Are you afraid of me, Elizabeth?"

"No."

"You know that last night with you, I was crazy. I was just so in love with you. I'm sorry. I'm sorry for what I did. It was cruel of me. I wasn't thinking."

I wondered if he was apologizing for the liberty he took with my body or cutting my hair or leaving me alone. In the last few days, I'd tried to blot out that night. I wanted to make it easy for us to go forward.

"Are you still married?" I asked.

"No."

"Do you have any children?"

"Just abortions."

I frowned.

"With women who couldn't decide," he said.

"Oh."

Frederick glanced up at the sun dappling through the trees. His throat was sandy colored, wrinkled, and the skin along his jawline was beginning to loosen. "Are you happy, Elizabeth?"

I answered *yes* quickly yet softly — a gate clicking playfully shut on the path between us — one that could easily be opened later. Seeing him again had stirred things up — the way the sea stirred up silt. It clouded my thinking. Reminded me of my past and the wish to be rescued.

"I'm glad you're happy, Elizabeth. A life is a terrible thing to waste."

He looked so sad that I wanted to kiss him, the way I kissed my children when they hurt. Maybe cunning men can detect this weakness in women. A woman like me, who had never been a natural mother, will suddenly mother a man. "Do you mean my life is wasted, or yours?" I asked.

He tapped his chest. "I mean me."

"Why is it wasted?"

"I have everything, now. I'm successful. I

have all the things a man is supposed to want: women, houses, cars, travel. I have the money to disappear."

"Disappear?"

"You know. Be elusive."

What might that mean? To spread out. To be free of people watching you. "Sounds nice, Frederick."

He crossed his arms over his chest, checked the circle of trees and rocks around us. "Not really."

"Why not?"

"I've missed the time line, Elizabeth."

"The time line?"

"Look at you," he said, "you're so young and you've done it."

"What have I done?"

He studied my eyes, lips. "You've gotten on track. You have a family. You're happy." He smiled. "You know, I had this fantasy of finding you here in a little cottage by the water. Just you and your philosophies."

Did I have philosophies?

"But you found me and my children."

His smile faded.

I looked down at the pinecones, thinking what a harsh winter might mean. How the bay could freeze as far out as Isle au Haut. It had happened before. One particular winter, the bay was a choppy bowl of huge chunks of ice, some as big as boats. All of Stonington became restless. Men tried to start old cars that hadn't run in years, children ventured out on the choppy ice that they'd been warned against, and mothers found rashes on the feet and hands of their babies. Bertie told me then that people here didn't like being separated from the sea. Stonington was a giant throbbing shell at the water's edge, she said. It needed the sea. It's the sea with which we're familiar, not the world, she said. I asked her if the sea needed us. Sadly, she said no.

Frederick moved closer, swept away a cedar needle that had fallen on my shoulder, then pulled back, admired my arms. "You're strong," he said.

I lifted one arm and made a muscle. "I'm a lobsterwoman. You know what they say?"

"What's that?"

"The sea isn't for sissies."

He smiled. "Really? You do that?"

"Sure. I love lobstering."

"I can't believe it. You're so beautiful. It doesn't really suit you."

What suited me? Was I still his Proserpine in the green velvet dress? Or had he made me into someone else? Painted his wishes over the sketch of me, the way my father would.

Frederick picked up a pinecone and tossed it a few times in the air. "Elizabeth, there's something I need to ask you." His face appeared more rested, almost tranquil compared to the other day, where in the bright sunlight, I could almost see the grid of city streets on his cheeks.

"What is it?"

"It's just something I need to know."

"What?"

He looked down at the pinecones in my lap, then threw the one he'd been tossing in with them. "Does your daughter belong to me?"

"Of course not." I laughed, trying to cover up my nervousness, holding that gate shut now with both hands. "She's my husband's daughter."

Frederick leaned back against the tree again, sighed. "Ah, then you did cheat on me."

"No," I said.

He looked at me, his eyes as serious as gray can be. "It has to be one or the other, Elizabeth. I looked your daughter's birth date up at the town hall. She was born seven months after I left."

"How did you know what her name was?"

"It's a small town, Elizabeth. Those things are easy."

I stood up, letting the pinecones fall away, dusted my skirt, then rushed to the edge of the cemetery, searching for my loved ones' gravestones. *Doreen Lee Johnson. Baby Girl MacDonald.* Watching them would keep me steady, give me a marker. *Red right return.* As soon as I saw the gravestones, they began to sway. Marin said that when he painted his swaying paintings, he was painting the *moving of himself.*

I turned around, put my hand out against a tree, imagining Frederick snatching Dorie and running off. "Why did you come here, Frederick?"

He stood up and leaned back against the tree casually, the way a man leans against his car after he's polished it. "I told you the other day. I came to take some pictures."

"Really?"

He didn't answer.

"Don't play with me, Frederick."

"Play with you? I'm not playing with you."

"Do you know how dangerous this is for me?"

He walked toward me. "Elizabeth, are you afraid of your husband? Of what he might do if he catches us together?"

"No," I said, "I'm not afraid of my husband."

"Then what?"

"I'm afraid of myself, Frederick. I'm afraid of what I might do."

"Are you not happy in your marriage?"

"Happy has nothing to do with it."

Frederick swayed in front of me. I reached out without realizing. He stepped closer, put his hands on my waist. Steadied me. "What is it, Elizabeth? Tell me."

Leaning in, I pressed my lips against his soft black T-shirt. It smelled like the wind. "I want to go back."

"What do you mean?"

"Part of me wants that place."

"What place?"

"My past."

He let go of my waist and gently scratched my forearms with his fingernails, reminding me how well he understood my body. Maybe it was simply the female body he knew, but for that moment, I let his touch belong to me, pictured it as something he had reserved. Everything with him was full throttle. While he touched you, he watched you, he talked to you, he listened, he smelled, he tasted. Being with him was to have all your senses hooked up to one motor. Being with him was to be convinced. "I've missed you," he said.

"Me, too," I admitted pulling back a bit.

Frederick licked the corner of his mouth, tilted his head and looked down at me, almost fatherly. "What is it?"

"She really isn't yours," I said firmly.

He kept looking at me.

"She's mine," I said.

Frederick closed my eyes with his kisses, then our tongues twisted together. He tasted of peppermint. His hands were still going up and down my arms and his body inched closer, until our legs and waists and chests all touched. He put his arms around me, made trails with his fingers over the back of my dress, up my neck and into my hair. Streams ran beneath my skin, weaving through twists and turns of memories: the soft feather bed at the great house. Linen sheets. His knowing touch, shadows on the stucco walls, bright moonlight, smothered sounds, warm sudsy baths, his hands . . .

We stopped kissing when a half-ton drove into the cemetery. Frederick pulled me into the trees, my mouth still open, my eyes still shut.

"Is that your husband?" he asked.

"No."

The red truck raced to the west corner of the cemetery. There was a small yellow backhoe sitting there, which I hadn't noticed earlier. Two men got out and took shovels from the back. It was Went Fallow and Tommy Fleck. We watched, Frederick's arms around me like rope.

"I haven't heard of anyone dying," I whispered.

Frederick parted my hair, kissed the back of my neck. "People die all the time."

I pulled away. "I better go."

He followed me. "When can I see you again?"

"I don't know, Frederick. I don't know if we should."

"Just one more time. There's so much I

want to ask you and I've brought some things to show you. Some pictures."

I kept walking.

"I have to leave tomorrow night," he called.

I stopped. It hadn't occurred to me that he'd have to leave.

Turning, I asked, "Where are you staying?"

"In the village."

"Where?"

"At the Inn on the Harbor."

"How come it's been so hard to find you? Haven't you seen me around town, looking for you?"

"Yes. Two days ago, I took a picture of you out on the pier. You were watching them load a truck with scallops."

"Really?"

"Yes."

"Where were you?"

"In my hotel room. I have a zoom lens."

I was confused then. I wasn't sure what it meant when a man from my past watched me through a lens, took pictures without me knowing. "Why didn't you make contact with me?"

"I wanted to be sure."

"Sure of what?"

"Sure of you wanting to see me."

"You mean you were waiting for me to lose interest? To stay home? Then what?"

"I would have left."

"Without talking to me?"

He took a few steps closer. "Elizabeth, you're the one with the ties. It has to be your choice."

I knew then I had surrendered something with this first meeting, shown him my hand of cards without even realizing, without knowing what they were myself. The grave-diggers started up the backhoe. It roared and rumbled, grinding against a chunk of granite. Frederick raised his voice, "Come to the pier tomorrow. I'll be watching for you."

He waved, a kind of slicing the air with his hand, an odd wave. In his paintings, Marin worked out a special language, an alphabet of marks that were recognizably like the things they symbolized and yet were a characteristic geometry. Water was suggested by written forms, trees were represented by wedges, the initial *M* was useful for making a forest or a sail, rake formations represented rain dropping from a cloud. Studying his paintings made me comfortable. His repetition of shapes was reassuring, in the same way that Michael's predictable actions were, his repetition of love. When Michael left the dock, he waved good-bye by smiling and saluting me.

I managed to sleep that night, but wild dreams tossed me in the bed. Dreams of explaining. I sweated, kicked and mumbled, making Michael so uncomfortable that he finally went downstairs and slept on the kitchen couch. This was a first.

"Is everything all right?" Bertie asked in the morning while I poured my coffee.

"Of course," I said.

The fuzzy coastal forecast was turned up. There were gale warnings coming in and Michael and his father were questioning whether Michael should tend the traps or not. Mr. MacDonald was mending a lobster net beside the stove. Sheila lay sleeping at his feet. Michael was at the table drinking his coffee. Usually, he would have been gone by now, but he'd overslept, which wasn't like him. I joined Michael at the table. He winked, continuing to talk. "It won't hit till later today, Dad, maybe even tonight. I'm going out, but I'll be back by noon."

"Make sure Jeb goes with you, son."

"He'll just slow me down."

Bertie put a plate of scrambled eggs and toast in front of Michael. He rubbed the inside of my calf with his foot, inching up and parting my knees playfully. "Did you finally get some sleep?"

I nodded, smiled.

Dana came downstairs and curled up on the couch. His pajamas were worn at the knees. "What kind of gale is it?" he asked, grabbing the weather guide from the shelf behind him.

Michael smiled, chewing his toast. "A regular bruiser," he teased. "It's swallowing people up from here to the Carolinas."

"It is not, Dad." Dana opened the guide, looked in the index, then flipped through its pages. "Let's see. Is it a moderate gale — *whole trees move; walking affected.* Or a fresh gale — *twigs break off trees; walking difficult; moderately high waves.* Or a strong gale — *slight structural damage occurs; high waves; branches break.* Or a whole gale — *trees uprooted; considerable structural damage; very high waves with overhanging crest.* What's an overhanging crest?"

"It looks like a row of thunderheads," Mr. MacDonald said, coughing up phlegm. "But it can be white with different colors beneath it. Red or orange. Prettiest thing you'd ever want to see, but mean."

Dana came to the table, scratching his bottom. "I hope it's a whole gale, Dad. Do you think it will be?"

Michael faked punching Dana. "We can hope."

He stood to leave and Bertie passed him his lunch basket.

"I'll be back for lunch, Mother."

"Just in case."

Dana hung on to his father's waist, dragging his feet while Michael hauled him toward the back door. "I'm a tree," Dana sang, "a tree pulled out of the earth."

At the door, Dana let go and looked out

the window. The sky was gray, a touch of yellow sunlight lurking somewhere behind it. The leaves were beginning to change, their tips orange and red. Nothing moved. It was dead calm. Humid. Muggy. I remembered Bertie saying before another storm that stillness was the worst thing about living on an island — it could make you feel abandoned.

Michael looked out. "It won't amount to anything for a while, Dana." He put his boots on, then grabbed his rain gear, touching all three of his children's life jackets. Not because of the storm. It was something he always did. His way of saying good-bye while they slept in their beds or played in the kitchen. He kissed my lips quickly several times and slapped my robed bottom. "Don't miss me too much," he said, pushing Dana teasingly aside and stepping outside.

Bertie was rinsing Michael's plate. "Maybe you should talk him out of going out today, Elizabeth."

"It never occurred to me, Bertie. Michael is very cautious. He'd never take a chance."

He was moving down the hill toward the water, his back tall and wide, his walk sure. Like a tree or a rock near the shore, he was shaped by what happened to him. He was not a dreamer, but a realist, his green eyes never shadowed but watching openly. Michael's ways came from experience. All his joys and heartaches displayed by his everyday choices.

"What do you think?" Bertie asked Mr. MacDonald. "Do you think we should call Michael back?"

Sheila stood, wagging her tail and lifting her face to Mr. MacDonald as if she were waiting on an answer, too. She could catch Michael by running down to the dock and barking. He always paid attention to her signals.

Mr. MacDonald patted Sheila's head, scratched her ears. "I think Elizabeth is right, Bertie. Michael won't take any chances."

"Oh, I know that," Bertie said. "But sometimes it's out of our hands. It's got nothing to do with careful. A storm has its own momentum." She dried her hands nervously. "He wouldn't be the first to disappear out there."

I told Dana to go get his brother and sister up. I didn't want him listening. Fear could travel through a home like fire and if the children got nervous now, it would be a long day. I thought of the superstitions of fishermen, the things they did to keep from disappearing, from becoming ghosts. Most of them wouldn't paint their boats blue or eat pork while they were on the water or whistle in their boats for fear of it bringing the wind. Obviously, disappearing was a curse for some and a luxury for others. Hadn't Frederick said he had the money to disappear? And did that include me? Could he make me disappear? My father could erase me simply with a glance or the wave of his hand.

"Bertie," I asked, "do you remember when my grandfather went missing in a storm?"

Bertie looked to Mr. MacDonald and nodded yes.

"Fifty-four," Mr. MacDonald said. "The winds blew so bad, they thought the big bridge was going to come down."

"Yes," Bertie said, "a lot of our windows blew out."

"Funny thing," Mr. MacDonald said, "there wasn't supposed to be any size to it. It came out of nowhere."

"My mother said Grandfather jumped overboard. Did you ever hear that?"

"He was good on the water, I know that," Mr. MacDonald said.

Bertie reached up, reworked her braid that was falling out, saying, "Elizabeth, that was long ago."

"Oh, I know that. I was just wondering what other people thought."

"It doesn't matter what other people think. A death is a death no matter what people say."

Michael had explained our marriage the same way. Maybe they went hand in hand, marriage and death, not in the awful slow bleeding way that I once thought, but with a natural shoring up, a clotting, which keeps things from escaping.

The back door shut. Mr. MacDonald was heading out to the work shed. Even though he wasn't yet strong enough to go lobstering, he worked at home, fixing the traps or painting the buoys or chopping wood. He was a man made uncomfortable by not working and a man made uncomfortable by most talk. He used to find solitude in milking the cows at the barn up the road, but he and Michael had gotten rid of the cows a long while ago, giving the leased pasture back to its owner. Michael said at the time, "There's not enough time to fish, farm and family. Something has to go." I marvelled at the way he used family as a verb.

Bertie went to the freezer. "I'd better roast something," she said, "the power might go out."

The children came into the kitchen, each retrieving cereal bowls from the cupboard and filling them with corn flakes. "Dana says the trees are gonna get yanked up," Vincent said, rubbing one eye.

"Oh no," I said. "Just a little wind. If that."

"Shoot," Vincent said, hugging my waist.

Dorie poured milk over her cereal. "Nothing exciting ever happens here."

Bertie dropped the frozen chicken into the

sink. It hit like a rock, rumbled and echoed. "Sometimes that's a good thing, Dorie. Sometimes just the day to day is best."

Later, the children and I waited on the dock for Michael. Vincent pretended he was a pirate, poking Dana with a stick, ordering him off the gangplank. The tide was coming in and water swelled and rocked the dock. Something was stirring, but the air remained still and birdless, except for the seagulls. Fishing boats raced frantically about the harbor. Several times, Bertie came down to the dock to see if we'd sighted Michael yet. "No," I'd say. "But don't worry, Bertie. The storm is a long ways out."

Bertie stared out, her face awash with the gray of the sky, then rushed back up to Mr. MacDonald, who was feeling weak and resting on the kitchen couch. He blamed his weakness on the low air pressure, but Bertie had scolded him earlier for overdoing it when he knew he should be resting.

"I can't lie around all the time," he had said.

"You'll be lying around dead if you don't take care of yourself," Bertie said. It was the first time I heard her harsh with him.

At two o'clock, the tide was higher. The wind was warm and playful, almost tropical, making it hard to take the pending storm seriously. Even so, I ordered the children off the dock.

"Why?" Dana said.

"Mom," Vincent said, "we're wearing our life jackets."

"Just get up here beside me."

It was on the way off the dock that Dorie noticed Frederick standing downshore. He was watching the swelling water, snapping pictures. He wore his safari jacket and what looked like a pair of black boots. City boots. "Look, Mom, there's the guy from the other day. Who is he?"

"Just a guy I used to know."

"Where does he live?" she asked.

"I don't know where he lives now. I didn't ask him."

"Where do you think he lives?"

"I suppose New York City. That's where he used to live."

"Whoa! New York City. I'd love to go there." Dorie took a few steps toward him. Frederick seemed to sense this and turned, then waved. I grabbed Dorie quickly. Too quickly. Obviously. "Watch the boys for a minute, Dorie. I'll be right back."

Before reaching Frederick, I said, "You shouldn't be here."

He shrugged. "Why not?"

"This is my family. They're asking questions I can't answer."

"I'm sorry. I thought maybe I'd missed you

down on the pier. I might have to leave earlier because of the forecast. I just wanted to see you again." He smiled. "Can we meet somewhere? Just for a minute.

"Not the cemetery." He grinned.

My mind raced over the village and its outskirts, its rocks and coves, the dirt lanes and the woods, finally landing like a bird on Helena's Ledge. The place Mother had taken me so long ago. It would be romantic watching the water and islands from there, glancing back to the village like something in our past. I could tell Frederick about Helena. We could talk. Maybe kiss. Touch each other without getting lost, if that was possible. In short, I wanted more of the other day, more cheating but at that moment, I had to get Frederick out of the sight line of my children and the MacDonalds and Michael, if he ever returned.

I could have wrapped everything up with Frederick right there, sealed it and sent him off, but I hadn't seen enough of him, hadn't felt his hands traveling over me enough, hadn't breathed in his fiery scent enough, hadn't heard the word *beautiful* enough. Besides, I had my own questions. Some people you could open instantly like a book, but not Frederick. He needed deciphering like the characteristic geometry of a Marin painting. Curiosity was my excuse.

The children stood like soldiers on the

little knoll, watching us. Hurriedly, I said, "Frederick, walk west of the village toward Sand Beach Road. On the first big hill over-looking the bay, you'll see Greenlaw Road on your left. Go to the end of that road. Just beyond a rundown house, there's a path on the left with a NO TRESPASSING sign. Wait on the path. I'll be there as soon as I can."

He nodded, looking back to the water, and snapped another picture of the circling lob-ster boats. When I turned, the children were pointing at the *Elizabeth Dorie* weaving be-tween the islands of Merchants Row, a white spray behind her. The boys jumped up and down. Dorie took off running up the hill. She loved to deliver news. She was always bringing the latest stories home from her friends and I suspected she created a few on her own. She craved intrigue, eavesdropped, called out questions of faraway places when we thought she was sleeping.

When the children asked Michael what had taken him so long, he said he'd forgotten that he'd moved the traps farther out to sea. "The lobsters are moving deeper early this year," he said. "A cold winter is heading our way."

He unloaded the boat, secured everything down, then took it back out to the mooring. We waited for him to come back in the dinghy, then we walked up the hill with the boys. "What's it like out there?" I asked.

"Lonely," he said without hesitation. I knew by that he meant still.

A lone maple leaf tumbled across our path.

"Michael?" I said.

"Yeah?" He put his arm around me as we walked. He felt solid and warm and smelled of those cooler deep waters. Part of me wanted to confess. To lay the whole story of Frederick out in front of him like a map he could study, carefully deciding a course for me. *Should I see Frederick? Should I just leave him out on the path? Waiting? Should Michael come with me?* Instead, I said, "Do you mind if I go to the library? I'm afraid they'll close up if the storm comes in and I'm out of books."

Michael knew I lingered at the library, had spent whole days there reading. He knew I could get lost in a book, lose track of time. He studied my face for a moment, almost looking as if he were about to say no, then said, "Sure, go."

We stepped inside the back door and I grabbed my yellow slicker. Bertie had put the chicken in to roast, making the kitchen smell of onions and sage. I took an orange from the fruit bowl, which was something I often did when going to the library. But that day, it was something I did to send a signal. Not a flare, just a detail to cover my tracks. I was already cheating.

It was easy to slip away. Bertie and Mr. MacDonald wanted to hear about Michael's day and the children were happy to be back home after being outside for so long. The house embraced them like fog.

The village suddenly felt small. Everything leaned in on itself, all the buildings, even the people as if they were walking into a constant wind. And I was suddenly tired, not just from the last few days, but from my life in Stonington, from the same old routines, the day to day, the superstitions, the gossip, the threatening weather. Everyone always bracing themselves. Who could win against wind or ice or crashing waves? All anyone could do was survive. Here we were, perched on granite that would still be here hundreds of years from now, barely changed by time. Meanwhile, we were beaten against the rock like birds in a crashing surf. Maybe places like this weren't meant to be settled. Maybe they would be best simply roped off and visited when the weather was good. Many of the out islands that were once settled were now abandoned. Shouldn't that tell us something?

Surely, other places brought more comfort to people. More conveniences. Places without the sea as their front yard or huge smooth rocks as their playground. My life might be better in another place. My children might like the city. Of course, they could visit their father and Bertie and Mr. MacDonald. Maybe like other children, they'd adjust. They'd learn to love two places.

They hadn't visited many places. Most of our outings took place on the *Elizabeth Dorie*. Michael always said why share a narrow road when you can have the whole sea to yourself.

Every year, we did take the children to the Blue Hill Fair and once we had driven on over to Castine to visit the lighthouse. From there, you could see Islesboro and the Camden Hills. Leaving Castine, we drove along Perkins Street, which ran along the harbor and was lined with big beautiful summer homes. Michael told the children that people came from New York and Connecticut, even as far away as Los Angeles, to summer in Castine. *What would it be like to be a family with a beautiful summer home?*

Dorie had her window down, watching the houses. "You mean they only stay in these houses a couple of months of the year?"

"Maybe just a couple of weeks," Michael said.

"Then these houses are empty the rest of the time?"

"Yes, they are."

"How lonely," she said.

"What do you mean, Dorie?"

Her chin was resting on her hands that were resting on the opened window. A breeze

238

blew her hair back from her angular face, her eyes ticking back and forth watching the houses pass. "All these big empty houses," she breathed. "It must be lonely for the people who have to stay."

"Yeah," Dana said. "I like Stonington better. It's lit up at night."

"This place is prissy," Vincent said. By that time we were driving past the public dock. "Look," he added, "they hardly even have fishing boats here. It's all pleasure stuff."

Near the rundown house before Helena's Ledge, caged dogs stood on their hind legs and barked from a steel pen. I hurried along, hoping Sid Billings wouldn't look out his window and see me. The dogs barked louder, furiously. Father used to warn me not to challenge a barking dog by looking into its eyes, even a tied or caged one, so I looked away and ran to catch the path.

Frederick had moved quite a distance into the path and was sitting patiently against a pine tree, his legs outstretched and crossed in front of him. The soles of his black boots were smooth looking. He rolled a tube of birch bark between his hands. A mountain of huge rocks rose up behind him. He stood up, hugged me. "Those dogs are wild."

"They'll settle down."

"Let's hope."

"What did you bring?" I asked, pointing to a brown leather satchel that was lying on the ground.

"Some pictures, like I promised.

"How about you?" he asked. Perhaps, he meant to say, *How are you?*

Still, I answered. "Just an orange, maybe you'll peel it for me later."

He touched my shoulder. "Anything you want."

He stretched his hand toward the ground where he'd cleared a small area of its twigs and branches and trash, making a kind of blanket out of the golden pine needles. Smashed Coke cans, cigarette butts and crumpled gum wrappers lay in a pile to one side.

"You're messing with sacred ground," I said.

"Ah, that's what's upsetting the dogs." His smile made the rest of him look younger as if youth, like fear, could spread through one's body, too.

We sat together.

"I saw your husband come in on his boat," he said, helping me slip my jacket off.

"Yes, he's back." *Where had Frederick been when Michael unloaded the boat? Had Michael seen him, too?*

"Frederick, I know you don't have much time. I want to ask you some things."

"Go ahead."

"Remember asking me about my daughter?"

"Yes."

"If she was yours. She isn't, of course, but if she was, what would you do then? Did you have a plan?"

"Well, if she was mine and you weren't happy here in Stonington, I'd take the two of you back with me to New York."

"You would."

"Of course."

"What about my sons? I have two boys. Would you take them, too?"

He lifted his shoulders. "I hadn't thought of that. They wouldn't really be mine to take."

"I know that. But they're mine. I couldn't leave them."

He shrugged again, looked away longingly.

Michael had taken Frederick's baby. And not just taken her, loved her, loved her still.

"I'm not young anymore," he said.

"But you can't expect me to divide my children up like candy."

He licked the corner of his mouth. "I know. It would be very complicated."

I decided to skip over the question. Release him for a moment. I could come back to it later. "If we worked the kid thing out, Frederick, and I came to New York, would you marry me?"

He reached out, rested his hand on my thigh. "I married you the moment I saw you."

"What does that mean?"

"Remember, that night you were hitch-hiking?"

"Of course I do."

He talked for a moment about that night, about the excitement of having seen me several nights in a row, running, then finally seeing me on the side of the road, asking for a ride.

"I was cold," I said.

"It was haunting. You stood so still in the car lights, and there was mist all around you. And you were white. White as a ghost with that beautiful dark hair flowing all around you. When you got in with me, you were shivering. You were like something wild. I wanted you instantly."

"But after all that, after you painted me all those times and we made love all those times, after you got me, you left me."

He leaned forward, lifted me easily toward him, sat me between his legs and wrapped his arms around my chest so we could both see the path that we'd taken to be together. His breath was warm on my face. "I was foolish."

Squirrels chattered and a truck revved up nearby. The tops of the trees hissed. "Look, Elizabeth, I love you. I can't change that. In my mind, I've tried over and over. I'd like to not love you. I wished those nights after I found you hitchhiking were nothing to me."

He locked me tighter in his arms. "But sometimes the memories of that time are more real than the life I'm living." He burrowed through my hair, kissed my neck, then asked, "What do you remember about that time?"

"How you made me feel things."

"In what way?"

"When you found me, I couldn't feel anything. I was numb."

Frederick rubbed his lips over my cheek. "What things?"

"Love," I guessed.

He whispered, "And you liked it?"

"I did."

"And did you like making love?"

"Of course," I said. "I don't understand why that kind of love is supposed to be a natural thing for a man, but a woman who likes it is bad." I thought of Gwen and how her desires made a whore of her to others. What right did anyone have to judge? To make her searchings as meaningless as names printed on a bathroom wall. I knew her, how she moved into love with closed eyes, how she trusted. There was nothing cheap about it. In fact, it had cost her everything.

We sat looking at the path and the trees, listening. Twigs snapped. The green around us was deep and lush, a hunter's green.

"Do you still paint?" I asked.

"Yes."

"Faces?"

"Mostly bodies, but I'm tired of painting bodies. I want to do something new."

"Like what?"

"Something fresh."

"How old are you?" I asked.

"Fifty-seven."

Thirty years older.

"You can't believe how fast it goes, Elizabeth. Every year a little shorter, a little blurrier."

"Do you think about dying?" I asked.

"I think about the time I've wasted and I think about the very end. You know how they say your life passes before your eyes just before you die?"

"Yes."

"I've thought about that. I think when I die, your face will pass before me."

"Why my face?"

He rubbed my cheek. "Because it's smooth."

"Smooth?"

"Your beauty is a kind of smoothness like water you run your hands through. You are very natural. Open."

A flock of swallows flitted above us, perching first in one tree, then another. Of course, they were seeking shelter from the storm, but it was also the time of year they gathered to go south. The very tops of the trees bent under the birds' weight. Beyond, the winds were beginning to grow, long and full sounding. Blousy.

"Tell me, Elizabeth, do I have a chance with you?"

"A chance at what?"

He struggled for words, then said, "A wholesome life."

I wondered if he planned to get this from me or possibly from being Dorie's father, and if it could include my boys. Women did it all the time. They packed their families up and they started new lives. My sister, Gwen, had done it over and over. Surely, I could do it once. Michael wouldn't want the children to leave. Maybe I'd leave them in Stonington for a time. And suddenly as if I had tripped over something, my mind went tumbling. I knew about a parent leaving. The loneliest I ever felt was when Father chose to leave us. Disappeared. Vanished. He didn't become a ghost, but he made a ghost of me. I faded, became numb. Even Mother's death was somehow easier than Father's departure. After all, dying was not her choice.

Frederick was looking beyond me in a general way, the way one watches the road ahead when driving for a long time. I looked down at the brown satchel. It was made of beautiful soft leather. Maybe kid leather. Probably the best leather money could buy. But it looked misplaced resting on the ground. The barren earth challenged it. The satchel would have been right at home in New York or maybe in one of those big summer houses over in Castine, but it was misplaced here. Lost. "Can I see the pictures?"

He touched the satchel.

There was a series of photographs, all beautiful homes he had built. The location of each was written on the bottom right corner in black script. Aspen, Colorado; Taos, New Mexico; Miami, Florida; Bel Air, California; New York City. Round stucco rooms, huge beamed ceilings, stone fireplaces, soaring windows, homes shaped like cathedrals. "They're big," I said.

"Monster houses," he admitted. "My clients don't know what to do with their money." There was disgust in the low ride of his voice.

"These places are beautiful, though. Who wouldn't want one?"

There were also some small pencil drawings: a series of naked women, some dancing, some sleeping, one looking at herself in a mirror and one staring into the painter's eyes vacantly and one photograph of a painting — a naked girl kneeling with her face in her hands, her long hair sweeping over her like a blanket, a high curving bridge behind her. "This is my favorite," he said. "It's you. It hangs over my bed in New York."

"It doesn't really look like me."

He studied it. "Sure it does."

"It has something of me," I said, "but it's

not really me. When people see the painting, do they ask who it is?"

"Some do."

"What do you tell them?"

"Different things."

I flipped through the pencil drawings again. "Are these all different women?"

"Yes," he said.

"Who are they?"

"Girls that reminded me of you."

The word *girls* was chilling. Maybe because it was said in the plural or maybe it was because I had my own girl now. Girls shouldn't be grouped together in a pile. Tossed about like sketches.

Frederick followed me to the foot of the ledge and waited while I climbed up the steep rock, hanging on to little trees that had sprouted through the crevices.

At the top of the ledge, there was a black duck sitting to the left of the rock, plump and facing the sea. A harlequin duck. Many times, the children and I had boated out to the Brandies and Roaring Bull Ledges surrounding Isle au Haut just to catch sight of a harlequin. They were rare. Probably because they hid in half-tide ledges and fished the violent surf breaking against the rock.

The duck didn't move. No doubt stunned by a wave he tried to take. For a few moments, neither of us moved. Being close to something wild drew me into a world I couldn't possibly understand or ever belong to for more than a few seconds.

Frederick hollered, "What's wrong? Why are you stopping?"

I put my fingers to my lips, *shhh'ed* him.

When I turned back the duck was gone, making me wonder if I'd really seen it. Maybe it had been a dream or even a warning.

Below Frederick secured the satchel between two large rocks.

"You won't believe what I just saw."

"Tell me when I get up there," he said.

The sky had rolled a deep navy, making the sea roll navy, sisters with the same urges. I guessed the tide was going out, but it was hard to judge since storms always brought some surge. The ledge was high, yet safe — the feathery treetops circled around it, embraced it, made a cocoon. Through the trees, you could see the village, but the village couldn't see you. Probably the reason restless teenagers liked to gather on the ledge. Way out, a large trawler was coming in. I hoped to find the duck riding somewhere on the easy current, but he was probably hiding in the deep wet rock below, feeding on the small crustaceans and snails that had washed in. The waves splashed and yawned below, lolled against the rocks.

At the top, Frederick was winded. "My God," he said looking out, "it's absolutely gorgeous."

And so was his face — flushed and gorgeous — watching the weather, checking the harbor to the left, the open sea to the right, his eyes reflecting Stonington like a rearview mirror.

Together we breathed the clean air the waves pushed our way — coaxingly — a rolling, hypnotizing sound.

"I want to build something right here," he said. "Is it for sale?"

I imagined Frederick tucked into the island, waiting. A rare bird. Me, being able to come to see him.

"You'd never fit a monster house on this little spot," I said.

He smiled. "I'd never want a monster house."

The wind tousled his hair lightly, like someone's fingers, and I reached up, touched its silkiness. I told him about seeing the rare duck. He didn't seem very interested. He simply watched the water. Still, I continued, "When a fisherman finds a dead harlequin floating in the water almost every bone in its body is broken."

He put his hands on his hips, looked at me. "What from?"

"From the violent surf banging it against the rock."

He shook his head, stepped toward the edge carefully, peered down. "There's a small ledge down there between us and the water."

"I know. There's supposed to be the shape of a woman in it."

"Really." He took a minute to study it. "I don't see it."

I chose not to tell Frederick the legend of Helena. If he wasn't really interested in a harlequin duck, how could he be interested in Helena? The duck was rare, but tales of abandoned and distraught girls were plentiful.

The sky was slowly darkening. Frederick stepped back, stood near the center of the rock. "I wish I'd brought my camera."

"Isn't it getting too dark to take a picture?"

"Not if you hold the camera very still and use fast film."

The ledge itself was smaller than I remembered — white-gray and as smooth as a beach rock, about the size of a double bed. The center of it rose up slightly as if a baby were hidden beneath the mattress. To one side was a pile of broken shells where the duck had been sitting. In the cracks of the ledge, there were little gardens of moss and tiny white pebbles, and a miniature tree that grew crooked from the constant winds.

Frederick reached back, took my hand and we sat in the center, facing the open water.

He put his arm around me. "This weather is such a turn on."

Lots of islanders felt that way about a storm and this storm like any other would bring its stories, the storm itself always being the main character, though, always holding its powerful position. People who sat in the path of these storms and came out unscathed began to think of themselves as lucky. Maybe even special for having witnessed it. For having survived.

"Do you come out here a lot?" he asked.

"Never."

"It's like no place I've ever seen."

He leaned over, licked the corner of my mouth. I closed my eyes, turned, let him kiss me. He laid me back, cradled my head in the crook of his arm. Two people in a circle of trees, within a wind, within a coming storm. It all whirled around us, slowly seeping into us until we were the beginning of a storm ourselves: touching, pulling, searching, writhing, whispering . . . For a moment, we teetered on the edge of unzipping, ripping, climbing, scraping, pounding, screaming, falling, then I told him to stop, letting him hold me instead. Once Gwen said that all in all, that was the sweetest part, the breathless resting after proving to yourself you were still alive.

"You're lucky," he said.

"Why?"

"To live here."

"Why do you want to take me away, then?"

My head was resting on his chest. His heart beat strong and steady.

"I guess I'm selfish."

I pulled up, hovered over him. His eyes were intense, clear as a piece of mica in granite. "Really?"

"Yes, but if you come with me, I won't be selfish. I'll give you anything you want."

"A monster house," I teased.

"Of course." He smiled.

I sat up, catching a glimpse of the village through the trees. "Frederick, what did you mean by wanting a wholesome life?"

He sat up, too. "I want to clean things up. Right some wrongs."

"Everybody wants that."

The sky had turned a muddy blue, kneeling low over the rolling water, which was now churning foam, the waves charmingly boisterous. "I can't find happiness," he admitted.

"Is that what you want? Happiness?"

He looked confused.

"Is it?"

Would he say that righting wrongs brought happiness?

He looked at the sky, squinting and admitting he was afraid.

"Of what?"

"Of not loving again."

A worthy fear. That fear of not loving again.

He studied the palm of his hand. "You don't know my life, Elizabeth. I've pushed all the limits."

"What do you mean?"

"I've had too much of everything."

Too much of everything? Would I be one more thing? Something he tired of like the drawings of all those bodies?

"But you haven't had too much love?"

"No."

The water was cloudy, churning at itself. "What is love to you?" I asked.

"You. Your shape. Your face. Your smell. The way your skin feels."

It started to sprinkle rain. The wind grew stronger, whipping my hair between us like ropes. "I want you to come back to New York with me, Elizabeth."

"I can't come with you, Frederick. I have a husband and a family."

He got up on his knees in front of me, gathered my hair, the same way he must have gathered it the night he cut it off. He twisted it behind my head and pulled my slicker's hood up. His eyes were foggy now, dreamy. "Come with me," he said again.

"I can't."

He held my arms very still in the wind, secured me like I was a camera he was looking through. "I don't want to be without you."

Behind him, the water was growing louder,

raging. Frederick squeezed my arms harder. His eyes changed. They were desperate looking, searching my eyes as if they were mirrors that could reflect some place between us.

I pulled away, backing up from the disappearing edge of the ledge, thinking he might do something desperate, he might gain momentum like the storm. Men hurt women they couldn't have all the time. What did I know of him now? How would a man who had too much of everything treat a woman who said no?

Putting my hands in my pockets, I squeezed the orange until my fingernails broke through its skin. Juice leaked out. I thought I smelled sweetness.

Frederick stood up, smoothed the wrinkles from his clothes. I sized him up: his blowing hair, the rain hitting his pleading face, his wrinkled neck, his flapping jacket, his strong veiny hands, his leisure jeans, his shiny boots. The same way he was probably sizing me up: my hooded head, my questioning face, my yellow slicker, my frayed jeans, my worn sneakers.

The wind was ripping, now, coming from all directions. The treetops blew and beat around us. The temperature was dropping quickly. I thought of hummingbirds hanging upside down in the trees.

"Elizabeth," he said, buttoning his jacket,

"I just want to be tender."

The word *tender* wasn't fresh coming from him, though. I knew the word. It was the way Michael loved me. With Frederick, *tender* had been wrapped and sealed long ago. Unwrapping it now was too late. It appeared spoiled. Tainted. He stepped closer. "Come with me. Bring your kids. I don't care. I want to take care of you."

I realized he wasn't listening to me — wasn't letting me say no and out here, on the ledge, things going wrong would simply be an accident. A foolish girl's poor judgment and it would cost me everything. Just like Gwen's attempts at love, at being rescued.

"Frederick, I can't leave here right now."

"Don't be ridiculous. You're a big girl."

Girl? Maybe that's exactly what I was to him. He couldn't see me now, couldn't hear me either. I was a memory. A painting over his bed. All these years, it had been so important to think someone loved me from those days when I was a *girl*. Someone who knew the greater world and still loved me. Someone out there, the way my father had been out there. Someone, who some day might return. Might rescue me. Take me away. *Isn't it every girl's dream?*

I took the orange from my pocket, rolled it in my hands.

Frederick wiped the rain from his lips hard, the way someone wipes away a taste they don't like. "I'm sorry, Elizabeth. I wish I was like your husband. I wish I was honorable."

"I'd better get back, Frederick."

He reached his hand out. "Wait, let me peel your orange first."

His face was sad, old looking. Defeated. "It will just take a minute, Elizabeth. Please. I need to do it."

I passed him the orange.

He braced himself against the wind that was whipping now, rocking him slightly. The pounding rain had soaked his coat, but he didn't seem to notice. He took his jackknife from his pocket, watching me, thinking. He flicked the silver knife open surely and then unsurely, he dropped the orange. Suddenly he was bending over to catch it as it rolled toward the edge, my orange, my coverup, my lie slipping away. He reached for it and missed. The wind was dark and smothering, pushing down. I knew better than to move, to try to hold on to Frederick. If he lost his balance, he'd take me with him.

Then, he slipped as if on ice and he was *off the rock.*

For a split second, Frederick's hand slid over the edge, then he was gone. The wind turned deafening, the sky sooty, the water black and hot looking. Marin painted the sun black on white paper. He said things were how you saw them. I got down on the rock, inched toward the edge on my stomach. Frederick lay facedown where Helena had lain, a lover over her, the water boiling around them. "Frederick," I screamed, but he didn't answer, didn't move. "Frederick."

Out on the road, rain poured down and the wind pushed me sideways. The caged dogs barked furiously. I should have gone to Sid Billings's house, but couldn't bring myself. What if Frederick was dead or already washed out to sea? How could I explain being on the ledge with a stranger? News would travel through the village like a breeze. A whore, they'd say. I needed Michael. He would know what to do. He would be tender. My arms and legs pumped frantically. My mind raced. *The tide will come in soon. It always does. You can depend on it. Set your clock to it.*

At the corner of Greenlaw and Main, a tree had come down with electrical wires wrapped around it like a snake. I knew even brushing against it would mean death. I paced back and forth in front of it, studying it, trying to figure out if parts of the wire might be camouflaged, but it was impossible to know for sure. While trying to decide what to do, I simply jumped over the tree and wire and began to run again, my eyes blurring, the rain hitting my face like needles, then bigger things were hitting me; maybe hail, maybe chestnuts from the trees or stones from the restless ghosts.

The storm was everywhere, turning the day to night. In front of me, behind me, hovering, hounding. I thought maybe I had run the wrong way. Maybe I was going toward Burnt Cove instead of Stonington, but whatever way it was, I had to keep going. I couldn't cross the wire again. I couldn't take another chance.

The MacDonald house lay nestled in its side hill, a yellow glow coming from the tiny windows. Seeing it brought such relief. *Red right return . . .*

They learn it by repeating, Michael said.
Like love.

Michael was walking up toward the house, leaning into the wind. "Michael, Michael."

He kept going. *This is my punishment. No one will hear me again. No one will see me. I'll move about this island like all the other ghosts.*

MICHAEL.

Just before reaching the house, he turned. Probably not because he heard me, but because he was still looking, he had not given up.

When he grabbed my shoulders, I was crying. "What's going on?" he yelled. "Where have you been?"

I panted. The way a woman does when she's having a baby, when there are no words for the pain that she will have to overcome. Michael steadied me. "I know he's here, Elizabeth. I've seen him."

Michael's eyes were no longer green but bruised looking.

"Michael, he's fallen off Helena's Ledge."

"What?"

"He's fallen off Helena's Ledge. Frederick has fallen off the ledge. He needs help."

"Is he in the water?"

"I don't know."

Michael looked out at the dock, rocking and pulling. It was inky beyond, invisible things crashed and banged on the water. "I'll get him," he said.

"There are wires down across the road," I said. "Be careful."

Michael started toward the dock, saying he wasn't going by road.

"Michael, you can't go on the water. You'll die."

"Get in the house, Elizabeth."

I grabbed his wet slicker, tried to hang on, but he kept pulling away. "Please, Michael, forget I told you. Just leave him until the storm is over. Please. It's not worth it."

Michael stopped, grabbed my arm. Held it up, the same way Father held Mother's the day she asked for impunity. "Go up to the house, Elizabeth. You've got three kids and

259

they're worried sick. Now go." He pushed me hard enough to make me fall back on the ground. Something flew past me, a bag or someone's shirt.

When I got up, the *Elizabeth Dorie* was already leaving, blurrily roaring up and down over the waves. Suddenly, I felt the heft of my future. A landscape anchored by guilt.

I took my slicker off, hung it beside the life jackets. Touched each of them.

The kitchen was full of ochre light and smelled of lamp oil. It could have been a painting. Bertie was setting the table and the children were putting together a puzzle on the floor. "Elizabeth," Bertie sighed, "finally."

She came toward me.

"I got caught, Bertie."

Her look was questioning. She sucked her lips in as if to keep from saying something, but her eyes said it all. They said, *Elizabeth, my love for you has limits. Stop messing around.*

The children gathered and hugged me. They were in their pajamas, which was a tradition when it stormed. It made them feel safe.

"Is it pulling trees up, Mom?" Dana asked.

"Yes, honey, it is. It's wild out there. Can't you hear that wind?"

"Michael's looking for you," Bertie said.

"I know. I saw him. He's checking the dock."

Mr. MacDonald was still lying on the couch with Sheila beside him. He put his hand up. I went over, brushed my palm against his, which was warm. "I'm sorry."

"No need to apologize, dear."

"But there is. I've caused you all to worry."

He squeezed my hand reassuringly.

Long ago, I'd told Mr. MacDonald about Sheila leaving me once to run with the coyotes. He'd listened carefully while I described her disappearance, and her return, cut and bleeding. "What made her do it?" I'd asked him.

"There's a pull in every one of us to run wild, Elizabeth."

"There is?"

"Yes. Some go out and never come back."

"Why?" I'd asked, but Mr. MacDonald didn't answer.

"You better get yourself dry," Bertie said firmly.

Taking one of the lit candles from the table, I went upstairs. The house was amazingly quiet without the buzz of electricity, just the wind whirling and banging outside. The candlelight flickered in the drafty hallway, but it didn't blow out.

From our bedroom window, I noticed several flashlights whirling near our dock. No fisherman ever left Stonington without another fisherman noticing, especially in a

261

storm. No one disappeared here without the tug of others pulling them back. I turned to see our bed sagging in the middle where Michael and I slept. There was nothing hidden there. It was the place we had made together, worn from years. *To be loved is to have your shore constantly washed with waves. It is erosion.*

When the *Elizabeth Dorie* came in, I rushed to the dock. The men were tying up the boat. "Did you find him?" I asked.

The men shone their lights in. Frederick lay twisted and motionless.

"He's breathing," Michael said, "but he's broken up pretty bad."

"Where'd he come from?" Pauley Johnston asked.

"Just a tourist," Michael said, "slipped off the rocks."

"No wonder," Pauley said, "look at them boots."

Michael directed the men in lifting Frederick, making a cocoon of our blanket to carry him up to the house.

"He was talking when I found him," Michael said generally. "Run ahead, Elizabeth, tell Mother we've got someone who's really hurt." The words were gentle coming from him, caring, as if he were speaking of a loved one.

Mr. MacDonald stood at the window with

Sheila. The men lifted Frederick onto the couch and the red blanket fell away. For a short second, Sheila growled. Frederick was shaking now, his head rolling back and forth, his face bloody, his lips swollen, his hands looking startlingly white beside him. Bertie scooted the children upstairs.

"He'll freeze to death," Michael said, "if you don't get those wet clothes off him. I'll get the car ready to take him to the hospital." He and the men and Mr. MacDonald shuffled outside, quietly. Clearly things that went on inside a house were not for them. They were for women. Decisions of care.

I knelt down beside Frederick, put my hand on his chest. His heart was beating fast, pounding. He murmured something about his chest hurting.

"It's okay," I said. "You're going to be okay."

"I'll get him some more blankets," Bertie said. "Try to get him undressed, Elizabeth." She handed me a pair of scissors. For a minute, I didn't understand the scissors. My mind went back to Frederick cutting my hair, to leaving me, then to me telling Michael to leave Frederick out on Helena's Ledge. To let fate take its course, knowing full well that for Michael fate was something that came along after everything else had been done. Fate was the result of life after you'd given your all. It was fearlessness.

I wiped some blood from Frederick's face. His nose was flat and floating, his eyes closed, and he was drifting in and out of consciousness. His swollen lips parted. Most of his front teeth were chipped. *The youngest part of him,* broken away.

"Elizabeth." He sighed.

Was he seeing me or a memory? Was he dying?

It was in the undressing, the removing of his boots and socks, the unbuttoning, the lifting and rolling of his body, the cutting of the clothes that I began to cry for him, or so I thought, but maybe I was crying for *the girl.*

Dorie snuck downstairs and stood beside me. "Who is he, Mom?" she asked with worried tears in her voice, her eyes on Frederick's bare chest. On his left side, a bone pushed out through his skin, a small white rib islanded in dark blood.

"Mom?"

"I'll tell you later, sweetie."

She rolled her nightie between her fingers nervously.

Bertie laid a patchwork quilt over Frederick, then put a stack of Michael's clean clothes on the floor. She got a warm cloth and held it to Frederick's face, wiping more of the caked blood away, then rested her damaged hand on his forehead. His broken teeth were chattering. I reached under the quilt and took his hand. Dorie went to the bottom of the couch and tucked the quilt around his feet, her hands appearing as light as wings. *Healing hands. Innocent hands. Sacred.*

Together, Bertie and Dorie and I became a quiet synergy, the total effect greater than the sum of our parts. Dorie's innocence, Bertie's wisdom and my physical strength. Maybe family *was* a verb, the motion of the best in each of us working together, moving forward.

Frederick began to breathe jaggedly and shiver.

"There's no time to dress him," I said. "He needs to go."

While Bertie alerted Michael, I reached for Dorie's hand and she came and knelt beside me. We locked our fingers together and rested them on Frederick, listening closely to his breathing. Dorie began to cry, somehow feeling the secret of us. There was no use in saying anything. We were in a language beyond words: the language of family. And as someone once said, anything said is already dead in our hearts.

Michael and the men loaded Frederick into the backseat. I didn't ask to go, afraid that if I crossed that bridge, I might never return. I'd be like my Father, letting fate wash over me like a wave, abandoning all the goodness that I knew. Why had I spent my life thinking of the people who had abandoned me — Father and Frederick — when so many stayed?

Like my mother after the skating accident, Frederick was immediately transferred from Blue Hill Hospital to Bangor where they could better care for his serious injuries. A few days later, Michael drove me inland so I could visit him. It was Michael's idea. He said, "I think you should go, Elizabeth. You have some decisions to make."

"What kind of decisions?"

"Elizabeth," he said, "you seem to think your life is somewhere else."

Frederick lay in a private room, much of his body wrapped. Even his head was bandaged. He tried to lift up when he saw me, but couldn't.

"Don't," I said. "Don't move."

I kissed him quickly on his lips, noticing his chipped teeth, which endeared him to me even more. "Are you going to be okay?" I asked.

"Of course."

"That's good."

"How did you get here, Elizabeth?"

"Michael brought me. He's waiting in the parking lot."

Frederick glanced toward the window. The

sky was bright blue. Clear. "It seems like a dream," he said.

"Your fall?"

"No, seeing you again." He glanced back, smiled. "The falling wasn't so bad. It was the landing."

A young nurse came into the room, her shoes softly padding the floor. "You finally got some company." She smiled, her eyes as blue as the sky outside and her cheeks flushed and smooth looking. "Are you part of the family that rescued him?"

I went blank, couldn't think for a minute where I belonged or remember if I were part of a family. Maybe I was simply an image hovering outside the MacDonald family just as I had hovered outside my own family, watching, waiting, hoping. The nurse seemed to notice my confusion. "Well, he's a pretty lucky guy," she said, jotting something on her clipboard before leaving.

Frederick's face was bruised black and there were several small cuts that were already beginning to heal. His gray eyes were watery. "Your husband is a lucky man, too, Elizabeth."

For a moment, I thought he meant that Michael was lucky for surviving the rescue, then realized by Frederick's sad yet intent gaze he meant by having me. Michael was lucky to have me. "Oh no, he isn't," I said.

Frederick smiled tenderly, a certain distance in his eyes. I knew there was no more question of me going with him. He wouldn't ask again. Maybe he decided on his own. He did owe Michael his life or maybe he and Michael decided it together on the ride to the hospital. Honor among men. Or maybe it was a deal Frederick made with the storm out on the rocks. An exchange for survival. He wouldn't be the first person to offer up his longings. If only I'd done that with my own life. Why couldn't I have philosophies? Ideas and beliefs that held me to my loved ones. Why had I run so easily?

Frederick's eyes filled with clear tears. I stepped closer, laid my head on his chest, lightly, afraid of hurting him. He brought his hand up and touched my hair, caressed it, then pushed my head snugly to him as if he wanted the shape of me to always stay there.

"I feel guilty, Frederick."

"Don't," he whispered, "it's not your fault."

"So many things are my fault."

"Feeling that way," he said, "is part of getting older."

I lifted my head. His eyes were different now, a warmer shade of gray, like flannel. "But I don't want to feel this way."

"No one ever wants to, Elizabeth."

I thought of those horses on Sable Island. The ones that Mother said craved a different life, having faith in the darkness and jumping into the night sea. "Why do we always think something is missing?"

"I don't know," Frederick said looking off, searching. A long cut over one eyebrow was stitched up messily and there was yellow oozing from it. It reminded me of the cut Sheila got so long ago when she ran off with the coyotes. She still had the pink and jagged scar. Sometimes even now, if I accidentally patted it, she winced away from my touch.

"Frederick?"

Clearly, a chasm was stretching between us as if we were in the ocean and gently floating away from one another.

"Frederick," I said again.

"Yes."

"Have you really always loved me?" I felt guilty for needing to ask, for the intention in it, but some part of me still wanted to know: the ghost of the girl, no doubt. The one without a weather guide for her heart.

Frederick started to lift his hand, but it pained him, so he stopped. I suppose he would have touched my face. "It's not right to say, Elizabeth. Not now." Then watching me very closely, he whispered, "You better go."

I fell away then, falling slowly like an over-ripe berry slipping from its vine. The same way I had fallen the day my father told me my mother would never skate again.

At Frederick's door, I turned back. He

smiled and winked sweetly. Something he'd never done before.

Before the cold part of that winter swept in, Michael had our new house built. A small Cape in which our children did sleep like squirrels in the eaves. He was just as loving and attentive with them, but *he* didn't wink at me anymore or slap my bottom playfully. Most nights, we slept together, but often I'd find him downstairs in the gray dawn light, that grayness that is neither arriving nor leaving. A grayness that can claim a place or a person, the same way a storm can.

He was usually standing at the picture window, looking out at the lily pond, a night mist hovering over it. Once, I stood behind him, massaging the cords in his neck. "I miss you," I whispered.

And he nodded, but said nothing in return.

I hugged him from behind. "I love you."

His heart beat steadily through his back, his body was warm and smelled of the sea.

"Do you believe me?" I asked.

"I want to," he said.

Night after night, I dreamed of men waving their flashlights from the dark shore so Michael could find his way back to me — I lay on high ledges and saw no one below — I rose from sleep to answer when he hadn't called my name — I stood at the window,

270

wrapped in a blanket, hoping for him to come home.

And what do I do when I wake?
I pray.
And sometimes I see my mother skating across the pond with her arms like outstretched wings behind her. Her long hair that never separated sways in the air with the glow of coal and moonlight and she is always smiling. January is when I think of her most, when the weather has stolen all that there is to steal and the earth looks barren under cold blue skies, as if waiting.

About the Author

Deborah Joy Corey was born in Canada. She lives in a small coastal village with her husband and two daughters. Her previous novel, *Losing Eddie*, won the prestigious W. H. Smith/Books in Canada First Novel Award.